DEAD WITHOUT A HITCH

A MADDIE SWALLOWS MYSTERY
BOOK 7

KAT BELLEMORE

KB PRESS

CHOOSE YOUR OWN ADVENTURE: MYSTERY OR ROMANCE

MADDIE SWALLOWS MYSTERIES

Dead Before Dinner

Dead Upon Arrival

Dead Before I Do

Dead Among Stars

Dead by Design

Dead in the Dark

Dead Without a Hitch

Dead by the Outlaw's Noose

BORROWING AMOR: New Mexican Romance

Borrowing Amor

Borrowing Love

Borrowing a Fiancé

Borrowing a Billionaire

Borrowing Kisses

Borrowing Second Chances

STARLIGHT RIDGE: Beach Romance

Diving into Love

1

My wedding day.

At forty-three years old, it was surreal—I'd never thought I'd be doing this again.

My twenty-year-old daughter, Lilly, shoved bobby pins into my hair as I sat in front of the long mirror in my bedroom and watched her reflection.

"You okay, Mom?" Lilly asked as she shoved in another one. "Sorry it's taking forever. It's the first time I've done a hairstyle as fancy as this. You sure you don't want Trish to do it? Or maybe you can go to the salon and have Debbie squeeze you in. You're getting married in two hours, and if I mess it up—"

I smiled, hoping it covered up the discomfort I felt from all the metal that was holding my curls in place. "It's beautiful, and there is no one else I'd rather have helping me."

Lilly pursed her lips. "I know you, and even if you end up looking like Frankenstein's wife, you'll tell me how amazing I am."

"Of course I will," I said with a laugh. "Because you're my daughter, and I love you, and I want you to be a part of my big day."

Lilly looked at her reflection and pulled on a stray curl of her own dark hair. My roommate and best friend, Trish, had already done Lilly's hair, pinning it into an artful pile on top of her head, because I couldn't handle something as simple as a ponytail.

"You have to stop worrying about my feelings," she said, turning her attention back to me. "I'm an adult, and I can handle some constructive criticism."

I often forgot that sometime in the last decade, my little girl had grown up.

"I'll keep that in mind," I said as she pinned up the last of my curls. I was still in my pajamas and hadn't yet done my makeup. I wished I would have learned all this stuff when I was younger. My friends had, but I'd never bothered to pay attention.

"Just one more," Lilly said, but it seemed to be one too many, and the bobby pin stabbed me in the scalp.

"Ow," I yelped, leaping from the chair. I pulled the bobby pin from my hair and threw it onto the floor. "I think we're done. We don't need that one."

Lilly ran over to me, another bobby pin in hand. "Yes, you do. Everything will fall apart without this one."

That was par for the course in my life—everything falling apart because of one stupid pain point that shouldn't make a difference.

"Fine," I grumbled. "But for the record, this is why I don't do my hair fancy. It hurts."

Lilly laughed. "You're saying the only reason you don't do your hair in a fancy updo every day is because of discomfort? Good to know." She was more careful this time as she slid the last bobby pin into my hair.

Once she was done, she handed me a smaller mirror so I could examine my hair from all angles. My breath caught. It only took one glance to know that I didn't need a hair salon—Lilly had done a truly beautiful job. And that was me being objective.

"Is this a dream?" I murmured, touching my hair. I couldn't remember the last time I'd felt not just pretty, but beautiful.

"No, it's not a dream." Lilly smiled and took the mirror from me, obviously pleased with my reaction to her handiwork. She paused as she turned back to me. "I know you've worried that Benji is too good to be true. But he's nothing like Dad. Benji is kind and funny, and he's your best friend. He's always there for you and Flash and me—you have nothing to worry about."

Yes, at one time I had worried. But not anymore. Just thinking about Benji sent butterflies exploding through my stomach, and I knew I wanted nothing more than to marry him. Even three hours was too long to wait.

"I'm very aware," I said, my smile returning. "Now hurry up and paint my face so I can get over to the church. Your grandma is probably losing her mind—I was supposed to be there twenty minutes ago."

Lilly gave me a funny look as she opened a drawer. "Paint your face? Who are you, Annie Oakley?"

"Annie Oakley?" I asked with a laugh.

She shrugged. "What? I couldn't think of anyone else from a super long time ago. Because no one 'paints' their face, Mom. They apply makeup."

How easily I aged myself. The funny thing was that no one had ever said they were going to "paint" their face when I was young either. I blamed all the old black and white movies I'd watched with my mom. "Well, I doubt Annie Oakley ever wore makeup, painted on or otherwise. Not unless it was with a gun."

Even as I said it, I knew it didn't make sense, but I was going to stand by my statement anyway.

Lilly laughed, even as she rolled her eyes. "Either way, you're going to be the hottest mom in that church."

"Of course I am. I'm the bride."

Lilly was just beginning to apply foundation to my forehead when the door to her bedroom burst open, startling both of us. Lilly jumped so high that I ended up with a streak of foundation through my hair.

She turned on her brother, who stood in the doorway, panting but smiling. "Flash," Lilly yelled. "Why can't you ever enter a room like a normal person?"

This was why it was hard to remember that my kids had grown—these moments. The ones where they still acted like they were twelve.

"I'm sorry, but it's an emergency," Flash said, though he was still smiling. Whatever had made him burst into the room, it couldn't be all that terrible.

"What's wrong?" I asked, trying to keep my voice level.

Flash looked confused by the question. "Why would you think anything's wrong?"

I blinked, and Lilly answered in my stead. "Because you said it's an emergency."

"Oh, right. I guess that makes sense." Flash did a little skip into the room as he glanced at me. "Grandma's freaking out because you're not there, and Dad just showed up at the church. They're already fighting about where he gets to sit—he wants a front row seat for the ceremony. She says he wasn't even invited, but then he proved that he was." He paused for a quick breath, then shouted, "Let the wedding drama commence," and pumped one fist into the air.

My son then ran out of the room but returned almost immediately. "Oh, and Grandma says she's mad at you for not answering your phone and if you don't get there in the next five minutes, she's going to murder Dad and the church will be a crime scene, and then your marriage to Benji will have seven years of bad luck."

"I don't think that's a thing—" Lilly started, but Flash disappeared again before she could finish.

I grimaced as I looked in the mirror, the foundation streak going straight from my forehead up through my newly sprayed hair. "However you fix this, you better make quick work of it. Your dad's life depends on it."

Lilly frowned as she spun the chair so I faced her. "Every superhero has their defining moment. This is mine."

THIRTY MINUTES LATER, I ran into the church. "Mom," I called.

My voice echoed in the empty space.

She wasn't there. No one was.

My mom had been here recently, though, evidenced by the extravagant floral decorations. The small chapel was filled with hundreds of daisies and yellow peonies. To me, it seemed a bit much, the way they adorned every pew and lined both walls, plus the front of the chapel. I had asked for simple, but I supposed this was simple for my mom.

As my gaze took in the chapel, I couldn't help the wave of disappointment that washed over me. It wasn't because of the flowers—they really were lovely. It was because I'd never imagined I'd get married in a church in the first place, and part of me felt like I was selling out. I hadn't attended church services for years, much to the chagrin of my mother and most of the town, but because I was a divorced single mom, they'd let it slide. Not without some grumbling, mind. But they'd finally accepted it.

But not have a church wedding? Not even Benji could get on board with that. He was a believer through and through, and I supposed that if marrying my best friend meant I needed to say my vows in a building I avoided most other days—well, I could do that for him.

I walked back outside and around the side of the church, where a large tent had been set up for the reception after the wedding. It seemed most of the town was here already, helping decorate tables with ceramic figurines or putting out more flowers. A stage was being erected at the far end, with full-size speakers. Usually the town used karaoke speakers, so this was an indication of how big a deal this wedding was.

"Maddie," my mom called from behind me. I turned to find her hurrying toward me, waving her arms frantically, like I could miss her. My mom had curled her hair, and she wore a beautiful yellow dress that matched the tablecloths and the flowers.

"You really went all in with the yellow, didn't you," I said.

My mom practically glowed as she surveyed her handiwork. "Just enough to convey that we're here for a celebration, not a funeral. It really came together nicely, didn't it."

That was one way to look at it.

Originally, I had asked for simple white tablecloths with black accents throughout the space—something that felt elegant. My mom had asked if I would mind a bit of yellow with the flowers and the decorations—it was such a happy color. Besides, she already had a yellow dress that would be perfect for the occasion.

Although hesitant, I had said it would be okay. It was easier that way.

I now regretted that decision. Sometime since I'd agreed to a splash of yellow, my mom had replaced the white tablecloths with yellow ones, but because the black accents had remained, the tent looked like a bumblebee had thrown up all over it. I pulled in a deep breath. It was fine. No problem.

Today was about family.

Speaking of.

"Mom," I said. "Flash said that Cameron has already arrived. You didn't scare him off, did you? The kids wanted him here."

"I don't see why it matters," she said, straightening an already-straight tablecloth. "It's not like he's shown up for the kids' birthdays or Christmas—"

I opened my mouth to protest, but she talked over me.

"Don't make excuses for him and say he's a very busy man. Yes, I know he's the head of the psychology department at that fancy university of yours. Yes, I know he's been on tour for the various books he's written. But the kids should be his priority."

Everything my mom said was true, and I wasn't about to excuse his behavior. But when it came to my relationship with her, I'd always had a knee-jerk reaction where I didn't want her to be right, and, even after all this time, I'd never quite managed to rid myself of it.

"He's still the father of my children, and they wanted him here," I said. "The fact that he came at all is amazing, and we should be grateful. The kids haven't seen him in nearly a year."

My mom harrumphed. "Fine. But he's not sitting on the front row. That is for distinguished guests—he can sit in the back."

"Distinguished guests such as yourself?" I asked with a slight smile.

My mom stood a little straighter and touched her hair. "Of course." And then she seemed to take me in for the first time, and she gasped in horror. "What are you wearing?"

I looked down. "It would appear that I'm wearing plaid pajamas. Flannel, by the feel of it. Very comfortable."

I knew that would rile her up, and it gave me wicked satisfaction seeing her mouth gape even wider. "But you're getting married in an hour. You should be inside the church, getting ready."

"It will take me five minutes to climb inside my dress."

A speaker crashed from the stage, and my mom whipped toward the noise. "Oh, dear. I suppose I'll have to be the one to deal with that." She eyed me again. "Maddie, I know you, and left to your own devices, you'd get married in those flannel pajamas."

Lilly and Trish approached us, looking like they were trying not to laugh.

"Don't worry, Grandma," Lilly said. "I'll take care of her." She looked gorgeous in a floor-length jade dress. If she'd been wearing white, our guests could have easily mistaken her for the bride, as opposed to me—the woman still wearing pajamas.

"I did shower this morning," I said, as if that were any consolation.

"It's true. She did shower," Trish said with a smile. She looked just as stunning as Lilly, her pink-streaked hair flowing down her back. It was the perfect contrast to her blue strapless dress. "But I agree with your mom. You should probably go slightly above and beyond applying deodorant." She took one of my arms, and Lilly grabbed the other. "We'll make a bride out of you yet."

Trish agreeing with my mom. That was a first.

"And what a lovely bride she makes," a man to my right said. I glanced his way and paused. I didn't recognize him, and yet there was something vaguely familiar about him. He had white hair and his fair share of wrinkles. He had so many frown lines that it made him look sad, even when he was smiling. My gaze traveled to his suit that had faded elbows and knees.

The man lifted a blue metal water bottle to his lips and took several long pulls from it. He lowered it and smacked his lips together. "I hope you don't mind me bringing my own beverage. I like to stay hydrated. Good for the soul."

"Not at all," I said. The sound of something shattering behind me made me whip around to find my mother surrounded by shards of broken ceramic. One of the table centerpieces.

"Mom?" I said, concerned. I tore my arms from Trish's and Lilly's grasp and hurried over to her. "What's wrong?"

Her gaze was frozen on the man who had entered the tent. "You're not wanted here," she said, her voice hoarse. "You need to leave."

"Mom, you have to stop kicking out our guests," I said, exasperated, giving the man an apologetic smile. I turned back to her. "Cameron was one thing, but honestly—" My words cut off when I noticed the way she was looking at him—like he was a ghost. My gaze jumped from my mom to the man and back again. "Who is he?" I asked.

The man chuckled. "You mean, she's never shown you pictures of your dear old dad? It's expected, I suppose, but still a shame."

My chest constricted.

Dad?

My father had come to my wedding? He hadn't bothered to come to my first wedding. Never reached out when his grandchildren had been born. I had no memories of even meeting the man. Ever.

Why now?

My mom straightened and placed herself between me and the man who claimed to have donated his DNA to my existence.

The man held up his hands. "I mean no trouble."

That may have been true. He seemed sincere when he said it.

But judging by the anger that had replaced my mother's initial shock, the man was going to bring nothing but trouble.

I needed to find Benji.

2
_____

My mom spun away. "I have things to attend to, and you are not one of them. See yourself out."

The man—my dad, apparently—chuckled. He looked at me. "Still the same feistiness, I see. That's one of the things I loved most about your mom. She always kept me on my toes."

"And then you left her," I said. It came out harsher than I intended, but my head was reeling. This was a man I'd been taught to forget. And I'd succeeded.

A woman with dark hair walked up, interrupting us. Her wrinkles betrayed her age—her hair was obviously dyed. She smiled brightly. "I finally found the bathroom," she said to my dad. She turned to me and eyed my pajamas. "Are you here for the bride or for the groom?"

When I didn't answer right away, having no idea who she was, she continued. "I appreciate what you're trying to do here—protesting tired traditions that expect women to spend hundreds of dollars on dresses they'll only wear once or twice, whereas the men can don any old suit and not be judged for it. Patriarchy, am I right?" She tugged on the dress she was wearing. "I hate these things." It was blue and knee-length with three-quarter sleeves. It suited her.

Lilly and Trish materialized by my side.

"She's the bride," Trish said, her lips pulled into a frown. "And she's just had a rather nasty shock."

The woman's expression opened, and she looked at me in surprise. "You're Maddie?" She gave an excited squeal. "I've heard so much about you."

Lilly folded her arms over her chest. "And we've heard nothing of you." She nodded to my dad. "Or him."

The woman's lips formed an O as she threw a questioning look to my dad, as though wondering what to do in this unusual situation.

When he merely shrugged, apparently at as much of a loss as she was, she turned back to me with a smile and stuck out a hand. "I'm Robyn. Your dad and I married... When was it, darling?" she asked, glancing at my dad. "Nearly four years ago now, wasn't it?"

He nodded. "About that."

She turned back to me. "That makes me your stepmother."

"And my grandmother," Lilly said, sticking her chin out. She seemed to have meant to make Robyn feel old—

wanted her to take offense. On the contrary, Robyn seemed to only be more delighted.

She clapped her hands together. "Keith, you mentioned that Maddie had children, but I hadn't realized how grown up they were." She gestured to Lilly. "I mean, honestly, you're gorgeous. A proper young woman." She glanced around the tent. "I understand you have a son as well. Is he here?"

Flash. In my hurry to leave the house, I hadn't bothered to check if he was dressed, let alone knew what time the ceremony was. Knowing him, he was eating popcorn on the living room couch while watching YouTube with his half-knotted tie hanging around his neck.

"I drove him over," Trish assured me, likely seeing my brief moment of panic. "I put him to work setting up the music for the reception, so he should be good."

"Thank you," I told her. If Trish hadn't moved in with us several years ago, I didn't think the kids and I could have survived.

I had mentioned this to Trish on numerous occasions, and yet, now that Benji and I were getting married, I knew she'd been feeling displaced. Like I didn't need her anymore.

It couldn't be further from the truth, but she had moved out of the house and into her own apartment two weeks earlier, and I worried what that might mean for our friendship.

I glanced toward the stage, and sure enough, there was

Flash, all dressed up and looking ready to go to a wedding. But he wasn't setting up music, like Trish had instructed. Instead, he was running back and forth across the stage, grabbing a variety of cords and light bulbs—ignoring the protests of those who had likely already finished what they'd needed to do, and now Flash was undoing it all.

"What is he doing?" Lilly asked.

"Probably syncing the lights and music for some big production," I said with a laugh. I couldn't help it. Flash had always moved to the beat of his own drum—and those drums often changed. Sometimes he played the bongos, sometimes the big bass drum. But always on his own terms. He'd be continuing that by moving to California, where he'd been hired to be a hacker for one of the biggest companies in the country.

I was so proud of him.

I turned back to my dad and Robyn. "I don't know how you knew I had kids, or how you even found out about the wedding. But you're here now, so you might as well stay for the ceremony." I held up a finger when they started to express their gratitude. "You will leave before the reception. Mom has been through enough without you stirring up the past. Especially today of all days."

My mom folded her arms across her chest and gave a satisfied nod.

Neither my dad nor Robyn looked like they were very happy about the condition, but they nodded.

"Okay, that's fair," my dad said. He looked at me. "At least let me give you my phone number. You know, so we can keep in touch. I'd like to see how you are doing from time to time."

Like my mom, shock was giving way to anger. "You had forty years to do that," I said. "And you missed your chance."

And then I spun away and stalked toward the chapel, all while searching my purse, frantically looking for my phone. I knew it was bad luck for the bride to see the groom before the wedding, and Benji had been busy dealing with his own parents.

But I needed to see my fiancé. Now.

As UNEXPECTED AS the arrival of my father had been, even more surprising were the tears that now flowed down my cheeks. I had no reason to be sad over this man. I had no relationship with him—had only heard his name mentioned in passing on one or two occasions.

Apparently, that had been two times too many, because when my mom had caught wind of the town gossip, she'd put a quick stop to it. After that, all evidence he'd ever existed had disappeared, like a wisp of smoke on a windy day.

But the tears—they came hard and strong, and Benji held me all the while. He'd immediately left home and rushed to me, much to my mom's chagrin. She'd said she could comfort me just as well as Benji could. More so, because she hated my dad.

That had seemed unhelpful, given the situation.

So here Benji and I were, sitting in a back room of the church, hiding from the rest of the town, who were no doubt filing into the chapel and being seated, even as I sat on a dusty floor, still wearing my plaid pajamas.

I forgot that I hadn't worn waterproof mascara—an oversight on both my and Lilly's parts—and I wiped at my eyes with the back of my hand. It was a good thing I hadn't put on my dress yet, because there were black smudges on my hand, which meant my face was even worse.

"I shouldn't care," I told Benji. "He means nothing to me."

I blamed hormones—darn perimenopause. And all the stress and excitement surrounding the wedding. And my kids leaving home in just a few weeks, venturing out on their own. It was a lot.

"Maybe it's the grief for him not being the dad he was supposed to be," Benji said, wiping away one of my tears with his finger. "You got used to not having him, and now he pops back into your life and wants to make amends. That would be difficult for anyone."

"Why now?" I asked. "Literally any other day would have been better than today."

Benji shrugged. "He's getting older and is likely feeling a lot of guilt for what he did. He saw an opportunity."

"Maybe," I said. "But it's not fair for him to spring all

this on me—on Mom." I buried my head in my hands. "Oh, Mom. She's probably having a worse time of it than I am right now. She was annoyed when I'd called you—said she should be the one here comforting me. I was so dumb to not realize what that really meant. She's the one who needed the comfort, and I pushed her away."

What a mess.

I pulled my hands away. More mascara.

I didn't know how I was going to get myself cleaned up and presentable in... I glanced at my phone.

"Benji," I yelped, jumping to my feet. "We're supposed to be getting married in fifteen minutes, and I look like I was just dragged out of the sewer."

He was already shaking his head, smiling, and he pulled me in for a kiss. "The sewer, really? Not one of the ninja turtles could look that good in flannel."

Flannel. I really was going to end up getting married in my pajamas, and my mom was going to kill me. I meant that in the most literal way possible.

A knock on the door, and Trish poked her head in. Her eyebrows popped up in surprise at the state I was in. "Not to rush things—I know it's been a traumatic day—but your mom is freaking out, and Pastor Franks says he needs Benji up front."

Benji didn't move from my side, so I gave him a little push. "Go. Trish will help me get cleaned up, and I'll be walking down the aisle before you know it."

He looked at Trish, as if asking if he could entrust her with my care.

"We'll be fine," she said, then finished pushing him out of the room. "Just stall for like ten minutes." She glanced at me. "Make that twenty."

The door clicked shut behind him, and Trish spun to face me. "I brought your makeup for touchups, so we'll start with that. And we're sticking with waterproof mascara this time. Next is the dress, then if we have time, we'll look at what we can do with your hair."

"What's wrong with my hair?" I asked, touching it.

Trish pulled a mirror out of her handbag and held it up in front of me. "Half of it is falling out of the bobby pins," she said. "But if we do it right, it will look like it was on purpose."

"Trish," I said as she worked on cleaning mascara off my cheeks. "I don't know what I'll do without you living with me and the kids. I mean, I know you'll still be in town, but these last few years—no one has had my back like you have."

Trish was quiet for a minute as she worked. "I can't take all the credit. You've had your mom."

"It's not the same, and you know it. My mom has tried hard to be there for us, but...it's different, Trish."

She finished with the makeup remover and worked on reapplying. "You're right, it isn't the same. But you have Benji now. You finally got your happily-ever-after. Maybe it's time I go off on my own adventure—find my own happy ending."

I held still as she applied the mascara to my lashes. "You make it sound like you're leaving Amor."

Trish didn't respond to that, and it worried me.

But she couldn't mean she was leaving entirely. She was my best friend. We had a therapy office we'd opened together. A life we'd built. She wouldn't just leave all that behind.

Would she?

"Makeup is done," she said, replacing the mascara lid and completely avoiding the question. "Now to get you in that dress."

Trish was right—this conversation would need to be put on hold. Benji was waiting at the front of a church for me. But it was a conversation that would eventually need to happen, whether Trish liked it or not.

THE ORGAN MUSIC BEGAN, we'd gone with the traditional Pachelbel's "Canon in D Major," and it filled the small church. I stood at the back, waiting for the doors to open. This was it. I was finally marrying my best friend. My pulse raced and my hands started to sweat. I wiped them on my dress.

There is no need to panic, I told myself. *You love Benji and want to spend the rest of your life with him.*

I bounced on my toes, wondering what was taking so long.

As if on cue, the doors in front of me opened, and I was met with pews filled with all my favorite people, and some not-so-favorite people. That was how things were in a small town. We loved each other, got annoyed with each other, and didn't always have a choice on how much time we spent with each other. But when it came down to it, we were there for each other. We were family.

Even Danielle Potts was there, our local sheriff looking beautiful in a knee-length dress, no gun in sight. If I wasn't mistaken, moisture had pooled in her eyes.

Danielle was crying at my wedding. The realization nearly made me cry, and I forced my eyes to dry. I couldn't lose my composure. Not yet. After the ceremony.

The yellow flowers that had seemed like too much earlier were now the perfect addition. My mom was right. Yellow really was the happiest color.

And then there was Benji, standing at the end of the aisle. Flash stood next to him, looking sharp in his tux. This was my boy, all grown up, and at my wedding. For all the good and the bad we'd been through, for all the times I had worried if Flash was going to make it to adulthood, or if he'd end up in prison because he'd hacked into the wrong server—he was fine. More than fine. Flash was perfect, and no matter how far away he moved, I knew he'd always come back. He'd always be my boy.

Lilly stood on the other side of Benji, right next to Trish. Lilly was my rock. My dreamer. She also kept me on the straight and narrow—reigning me in when my anxiety got the best of me and made me a little bonkers. Those three standing up there together, waiting for me to walk towards them—there couldn't have been a more perfect moment.

Whatever pictures our photographer took of the event, this was going to be my favorite memory. The one that I would keep with me always.

My mom took my arm—she'd be the one giving me away at my wedding. Not my father. Not my ex-husband, who was watching me from the second row from the back. My mom, who it had taken me twenty years to return home to.

It had been twenty years too long.

The aisle felt much longer than it had the few times I'd been inside the church. I avoided my father's gaze as I passed him and instead focused on my family.

And then I was there. With Benji. And nothing else mattered. No one else mattered.

It was just him and me.

Benji smiled down at me, his eyes conveying more than words ever could.

He loved me. And we were going to conquer the world together.

I was tempted to tell Pastor Franks to hurry things

along—Benji and I had a honeymoon to get to—but then my father had to go and ruin everything when he started screaming.

3

No. This couldn't be happening. I wasn't going to allow it. I wanted one moment to be mine. One moment that was perfect and wonderful and the start to my new beautiful life.

And the one person who wasn't supposed to be here was taking that away from me.

More screaming. It shattered the peace I felt—the pure, unadulterated happiness I'd had for all of five minutes.

I spun toward the pews in time to see my father stumble out into the aisle, his wife, Robyn, chasing after him. His arms flailed and he smacked her in the head. She stumbled backwards, but he didn't appear to notice as he collapsed onto the ground. His body stilled, and the rest of the guests stared in stunned silence.

"Really, Keith," my mom said, jumping to her feet. Her

eyebrows were drawn, her hands clenched. I could feel the anger radiating off her. "After all these years, you haven't changed one bit—still half-drunkenly stumbling your way through life. And at your daughter's wedding, no less." She looked at Robyn. "If I were you, I'd walk out of here and never turn back. You're too nice for the likes of him."

Robyn ignored my mom and dropped to her knees, taking my father's hand in hers. She stared helplessly at his figure, his breathing labored. "He's not drunk. He's been sober for twelve years."

"You've only been married for four," my mom spat out, seemingly trying to catch Robyn in a lie.

"But I've known him for seven. I've never seen him have a drink in all that time."

My mom was already shaking her head. "I know what Keith looks like drunk, and this is it."

Robyn turned to me, tears cascading down her cheeks. "Please, believe me. Keith wouldn't do anything to jeopardize meeting you. He's been preparing for this day since long before I met him. Hasn't stopped talking about it. Hasn't stopped working towards becoming the man he needed to be."

I didn't want to hear it. I didn't want her to tell me what a good man my father had become.

Because that meant I'd need to help him. I would need to pick his sorry drunken self off the floor, in my wedding dress no less, and I would need to help get him sober.

Because, for better or worse, he was my father.

And apparently, according to Robyn, a good man, though at the moment I was struggling to see it.

"Let's get him outside," I said, stepping forward.

Danielle Potts had already moved from her pew and into the aisle. She approached my father cautiously. She held up a hand to me. "Stay where you are, Maddie."

"He's just passed out," I said, taking another step forward.

She shot me a look that told me she was serious—I really needed to stop.

And I did.

"Did he look drunk to you?" the sheriff asked, bending down and placing two fingers on the inside of my dad's wrist. She was checking his heart rate.

I wanted to say yes, because that was the easy answer. The answer that allowed me to stay mad at him. But I shook my head no. "He seemed like he was in pain. Like he was scared."

Danielle nodded, slowing standing. "It looked like that to me too."

"But he was sitting right here, next to me," Robyn said, her voice rising in volume. She had been concerned before —confused, even. But now she was panicked, her gaze darting all over the room. "I don't understand. All he had was water." She pointed to the blue bottle he'd been carrying earlier. It still sat on the church pew.

Danielle pulled a handkerchief out of her purse and used it to pick up the bottle, then unscrew the lid. She sniffed it, then reared back. "That's not water," she choked out.

Robyn collapsed onto the bench, her expression stunned. "He said he didn't drink anymore. I believed him —never questioned why he brought that tacky water bottle with us everywhere."

"It's not alcohol either. At least, if it is, it's not the only thing in there." Danielle carefully screwed the lid back on and bent back over my father. She once again placed her fingers on his wrist, then, after a long moment, glanced around the chapel. Her gaze settled on the far side of the room, middle pew. "Dr. Harris, we're going to need your services."

Robyn looked at the sheriff. "I don't understand."

Danielle hesitated, and I noticed that my father's chest was no longer rising.

"I'm sorry, Robyn," she said, "but he's dead."

Pastor Franks suggested we could continue with the wedding ceremony after Dr. Harris had taken away my father's body—Dr. Harris was both our doctor and coroner —but I was the first to object. Not only would that be incredibly inappropriate and cruel to Robyn, but this was not how I wanted to remember my wedding day. Of course, it didn't matter if Benji and I got married today, next week, or ten years from now—today's events would be impossible to forget. I could still hear my father's screams.

"Honestly, I just want to go home," I said. "I need some time to process what has happened here. I'm sure everyone else would like the same."

Danielle raised a finger. "Unfortunately, that will need to wait." She then moved to the front of the chapel and turned to face the restless crowd. "I know this isn't ideal, but I'm going to need everyone to stay where they are for a while longer. Bride and groom included. I'll be calling you each individually into one of these back rooms to answer a few questions. You can go home once you've had your turn."

I'd been around long enough to know what that meant.

The sheriff wasn't treating this as an accidental death. She was treating this as a murder.

I wasn't the only one who recognized it for what it was.

The entire room now erupted in protests.

"But no one knew Keith," my mom said, protesting loudest of all.

"It seems that way, doesn't it," the sheriff said, glancing at her. "As far as I know, you and Robyn are the only ones at this wedding who knew your ex-husband. And he died under suspicious circumstances. I'm sure I don't have to tell you what position that puts you in."

For once, my mom was speechless. She opened her mouth but then quickly closed it again.

"However, you and Keith lived here together when Maddie was a baby," Danielle continued. "Which means there is the possibility that someone else in town could

offer valuable information. I'm sure you'd prefer a tempo-
rary inconvenience rather than me driving my obvious
choice of suspects down to the station."

My mom nodded, mute.

"Great." Sheriff Potts turned back to the room.
"Because it's Maddie's special day, let's start with the
bride."

I wasn't sure that was an honor I wanted, but I decided
to show Danielle I could be a good sport, and I followed
her into the back.

I hesitated when she led me into the room I had
previously dressed in. The room where I had cried on
Benji and smeared my makeup because I had just met a
father I had always thought wanted nothing to do
with me.

"Danielle, if it's all the same to you, I'd prefer a
different room. You see—"

She didn't wait for me to give an explanation. "I'm
sorry, Maddie, but I don't have time for this. Keith Lawson
either came all the way to Amor to meet you on your
wedding day, only to then kill himself, or he was
murdered."

I stared at her bluntness. "How did you come to that
conclusion? Dr. Harris hasn't even removed the body yet,
let alone done an autopsy. My father could have died from
natural causes—he was an alcoholic, after all."

"There were burn marks—blisters—on his lips. Like
he drank acid," Danielle said. "That, and the liquid in his

water bottle was super strong. Like bleach or some kind of cleaner. I won't know until I have it analyzed."

His blue water bottle. That he, apparently, took with him everywhere he went. How long had he been doing that? Since he'd lived here forty years ago? Or more recently?

"I don't think he killed himself," I said. "Robyn said he'd been working really hard so he could come back to Amor—that he wanted to be a part of my life. He knew about me—about my kids. He wanted to meet his grand-children. Why would he do that if—"

"—he planned to commit suicide at your wedding," Danielle finished. "Yes, I agree. You had a better vantage point than me—you could see everything from the front of the chapel. Do you remember who he was sitting by, other than Robyn?"

Oh, that was why the sheriff wanted to speak to me first. She thought I'd seen something.

"I don't know," I said, trying to remember. It was all a blur. For some reason, the only thing I could think of was yellow flowers. The sheriff crying at my wedding. When I'd walked down the aisle, I had noticed my father and Robyn, but I'd avoided their gazes.

Next to my father had been... "Dale Montgomery. My father was sitting next to the aisle, and Dale was sitting next to Robyn. He owns the custard stand over by the park. He didn't kill my father, though."

"How do you know that?" Danielle asked, already

writing in her notebook that she'd pulled from her handbag. It seemed she took that thing with her everywhere. Even weddings.

"Because he's barely older than me. Why would he kill my dad if he wouldn't even remember him? I lived with Keith, for crying out loud, and don't remember him."

The sheriff shrugged. "Point taken."

"Besides, whoever killed my father wouldn't be someone who was sitting next to him during the ceremony," I continued. "They tampered with his water bottle—a bottle they knew he took with him everywhere. They had to have done that between the time he arrived at the church and when everyone was seated for the ceremony. That means your murderer had at least an hour to get the job done. It could have been just about anyone."

Danielle stopped writing. "I really wish you wouldn't have made such a good point," she said, and placed her notebook and pen back in her handbag. She settled back into her chair and studied me, her expression curious. "I have to ask, did you have any reason to harm your father?"

And so it began.

"No, I didn't. My mother never talked about my father. All I knew was that we were better off without him, and I learned not to ask more than that."

Danielle released a long breath. "That is tough, and then to have him show up today of all days. I can't imagine what you must be going through right now."

"What I'm going through, Danielle, is that today is my

wedding day," I said, my frustration obvious, despite my best efforts. "And I'm supposed to be married already. Instead, I'm here talking with you about suspects for the murder of my father whom I hadn't met until two hours ago." I shook my head. "I watched him die."

"Which is why it is so important that you tell me anything you remember," Danielle said. "Even the smallest detail could help me solve this quickly and give you the closure you deserve."

I laughed, but it was devoid of humor. "You think anything in my life is that easy? It took twenty years for my first marriage to fall apart, and another five years for me to admit that I was in love with my childhood best friend. It took my father forty years to get his life in shape enough to come out for a visit. And murder investigations? Well, nothing has come easy, has it? Every investigation I've been a part of has involved an innocent person nearly going to jail before we've managed to solve it. We cut it too close every time. And now you think the investigation of a man being murdered, a man no one has seen in forty years, is going to lead to a swift conclusion?"

"There is one person who has spent time with him more recently than that," Danielle said, her voice quiet.

Yes. Robyn. My stepmother.

"She didn't do it," I said. "Though I wish she had. Would make things a lot easier."

Danielle's eyebrows popped up in surprise. "That's very

unlike you, Maddie, wishing for someone to have killed your father. And someone as nice as she is, as well."

I sighed and held up my arms. "Look at me, Danielle. I've had my makeup and hair done twice today because I keep ruining it, and I'm being questioned by our sheriff while wearing a wedding dress. I should be dancing and eating little finger sandwiches and smashing a piece of wedding cake in Benji's face. I'm sorry if my patience is running a bit thin today."

Danielle's eyes filled with the one emotion I couldn't stand—pity. But before I could call her out on it, Flash and Lilly burst into the room, making us both jump.

"You can't arrest our mom. It was us. We killed our grandfather," they said at the same time.

Thankfully, Danielle had been around both of my kids enough that she knew better than to take anything they said at face value.

She folded her arms across her chest and leaned back in her chair. "Why?"

Flash and Lilly both gave her blank looks.

"What do you mean?" Lilly said. "He left Grandma forty years ago, he ruined Mom's wedding—the real question is, why not?"

Both kids were avoiding my gaze, which meant they knew I wouldn't approve. I assumed this was a ploy to get me off the hook for my father's murder. They must have assumed the sheriff actually thought I had done it.

Danielle gave a little nod, like she'd expected as much.

"I appreciate your honesty. I'll just need a written statement from both of you, and we can move forward with setting a court date. I might be able to get you some leniency because you are young and you confessed to the murder before I had any evidence. It won't be much, of course, because...well, you murdered someone. You have no priors, though, so that should help."

Lilly and Flash looked at each other, panic exploding across their features.

"But...you can't arrest two people for one murder," Flash protested.

I could tell it was taking the sheriff everything in her to not burst out laughing, and I had to admit, with the looks on my kids' faces, I was having similar trouble.

"Let me guess," Danielle said. "You watched a movie where multiple people confessed to the same crime, and because the detective couldn't prove which one of them had actually done it, the detective had no choice but to release all of them."

Flash nodded vigorously. "Exactly."

That earned a punch in the arm from Lilly. "Idiot."

His lips formed a small O, and then he looked at me with a scowl, already beating himself up for his mistake. "Sorry, Mom. We really thought that would work."

"No, *you* thought it would work," Lilly said. "I told you the sheriff would see right through it."

Danielle let her smile break through. "Now that I have you two here, why don't you have a seat? I have some questions for you." She glanced at me. "Go home, Maddie. Get some rest. We'll talk more later."

I stared at Danielle until her gaze met mine. "You aren't questioning my children. Not without me here."

Danielle didn't look away. "I can question them without you here, and I will."

She then motioned to the door, indicating that our time was finished.

I didn't like leaving my kids in there with Danielle, alone. But I also trusted everyone in that room. I trusted my kids to hold their own, and I trusted Danielle to be kind and fair when questioning them. If anything, Flash and Lilly would be the ones with the information by the end of the interrogation.

In fact, I was counting on it.

4

When I left my kids with Danielle, Benji was waiting for me outside the room. I made a beeline towards him, and he gathered me in his arms.

"You okay?" he asked, his words muffled against my hair.

That was a difficult question.

I fought back tears. "My father is dead, people think my mom killed him, my kids are being interrogated by Sheriff Potts, and you and I are still not married—but yeah. Sure. I'm fine."

Benji pulled back and tucked a lock of hair behind my ear. "I'm sorry. Today—it's not gone well, has it? If it's any consolation, no one thinks your mom killed Keith."

That was a first. Usually, the town mob immediately assumed it was my family who were the culprits. We were a bit too opinionated and outside the box for their liking.

Thankfully, the town realized how much they needed the therapy office that Trish and I had opened, and had subsequently determined that our other idiosyncrasies were forgivable.

But my being a therapist also meant that many people avoided me whenever possible, because they had talked about things in my office that they would never confess elsewhere. They were either embarrassed by it or afraid that I was going to tell others, despite my assurances that I would never do such a thing.

"Okay, if not my mom, who do they think did it?" As soon as I said it, I already knew. "Robyn."

Benji nodded. "She's the outsider. She's the one they don't know. And anyone who watches crime dramas knows that it's always the wife who did it."

Which my mom had been. But not anymore. A new woman had replaced her. A woman who knew a lot more about us than we knew about her. And, even though it didn't make sense, that meant we couldn't trust her.

"Maybe Robyn did do it," I said. "Maybe she was unhappy that my dad was traveling out here to visit his other family—maybe it bothered her that he wanted a relationship with us. What if the ex-wife—my mom—saw that he had changed, and she wanted him back. What then? Maybe that's why Robyn came with him."

Footsteps alerted me to someone walking the hallway behind me. Benji's concerned expression turned to embarrassment when he glanced behind me, and I immediately knew who had joined us.

"I didn't mean to eavesdrop," Robyn said as I turned to face her. "Dr. Harris just took Keith and I wanted to go with him, but I was told the sheriff wanted to see me." She paused. "You've got it all wrong. I wanted Keith to come out here. In fact, I encouraged him." Her eyes were puffy, like she'd been crying. Of course she had. Her husband had just been murdered, and everyone thought she'd done it. Her gaze dropped. "I had the opportunity to see the Keith who was a loving, funny, and wonderful husband. You didn't. I told him he should come out here for the wedding, but he was nervous about meeting you, and he asked if I'd join him."

Heat traveled up my neck and into my cheeks. "I'm sorry you heard that. I didn't mean—"

Robyn held up a hand, stopping my bumbling excuses before I could make things worse. "It's fine. Really. I get it. I'm the random woman who has catapulted into your lives, and now you don't know what to do with me."

My thoughts exactly, though I wasn't going to tell her as much. That also reminded me of another problem we had.

"Are you staying at the hotel?" I asked.

She nodded. "Newly renovated, right? It's gorgeous."

"And it's not safe," Benji said, realizing what I was thinking. "I would invite you to my house, but I already have family staying with me. They flew in for the wedding —" His eyes widened. "I totally forgot about them. They're still sitting out there with everyone else, probably beside themselves, wondering what's going on. They come to town for my wedding, and instead they're involved with a murder investigation."

Annoyance bubbled up in my chest.

Annoyance at Keith and Robyn for choosing today of all days to re-enter my life. Annoyance at whoever couldn't put their grudges aside for just one day and not kill someone at my wedding.

Benji recognized my emotional shift, but he mistakenly thought my annoyance was directed at him. "We're going to get married," he said, his voice firm as he took my hands in his. "Today doesn't change that. But it's not going to be under these circumstances."

"So what, we're supposed to put everything on hold until we find this guy?" I asked. "Do you realize how many times that has happened over the past several years? If we continue to put our lives on hold every time we find a dead body, we'll never get anything done—never go anywhere."

Robyn held up a hand, as if she were back in school. "I'm assuming that's a figure of speech. Or at least an exaggeration."

Benji grimaced. "You'd think so, but no. Unfortunately, this happens quite a lot with Maddie."

Robyn took a step away from me, like just being

around me was enough to condemn her to an early death. Like I carried the plague. I didn't blame her—even I'd wondered from time to time if I was cursed.

But one glance at Robyn—one look at the sadness she carried with her—and I knew what had to be done. And yes, it meant putting my and Benji's life on hold.

"Would you like to stay with me, Robyn? My son can sleep on the couch, and you can take his bed. Don't worry, I'll have him change the sheets."

I expected Robyn to be grateful. To say thank you, and how could she ever repay me?

Instead, she frowned. "I already have someplace to stay."

"Yes, I know," I started, wondering how to put this delicately. "But the thing is, you are no longer just a guest at our wedding. You're the wife of...a murder victim. It changes things."

"What does it change?" she asked, like she genuinely didn't understand what I was getting at.

Benji tried this time. "Small towns, they're different than other places. People talk, you see. Nothing stays quiet. Nothing is ever private, even when it should be."

Robyn's expression opened in understanding. "You're afraid there will be reporters hanging around the hotel, wanting to talk to me. Paparazzi. That kind of thing."

"We don't really have those kinds of reporters in Amor," I said. "But we do have nosy people. And..." I paused—this was taking forever. I just needed to come right out and say it. "Robyn, they think you did it. That you killed Keith. And you staying at the hotel by yourself... I love the people in this town. Most of them. I really do. But they are wildly protective. They might not have known Keith, but they do care if a murderer is staying in their hotel."

This time Robyn really did understand. "You aren't worried whoever killed Keith will come after me. You're worried your town will."

"That about sums it up," Benji said, looking truly sorry about it. "I wish I could say that we're better than that. But people in our town aren't exactly welcoming to those they don't know. Their trust has to be earned. And I'm afraid, through no fault of your own, you've gotten off to a rocky start."

Robyn looked from me to Benji. "No."

I glanced at him, silently asking what we were supposed to do now.

"Mrs. Lawson—" Benji started.

"Carter," she interrupted. "I kept my last name. And if I stay with you—or anyone else, for that matter—then you are guilty by association. And I can't have that on my conscience. Besides, you are a nearly newlywed couple. You can't start your marriage with a houseguest. I believe in omens, and that is a terrible one."

Robyn was full of surprises. If Keith—my father—had

managed to convince a woman who was this good to marry him, maybe he really had changed.

"At least let the sheriff assign her deputy to watch over the hotel and make sure there's no trouble," Benji said. "Just to be safe."

Robyn gave us both a long look. "I'll think about it."

The door to the back room opened, and Flash and Lilly came bounding out, looking excited. The sheriff—not so much. She looked like she'd just been put through the wringer.

"I'm going to have to save everyone else for later today," she told us, her voice tired. "I'll need the names of everyone who attended the wedding. I'm assuming you have a list of all guests."

Whatever the kids had done to her, it must have been bad.

I nodded. "Yes."

Danielle's gaze landed on Robyn. "Including those who weren't invited?"

I gave another nod but couldn't help but notice Robyn's fallen expression. Even to Danielle, who had once been an outsider herself, Robyn didn't belong.

"Leave your contact information with my deputy before you go," she told Robyn, and then she disappeared down the hallway and around the corner, likely to let everyone else know they could leave.

Flash turned to us, his eyes lit up in excitement. "We got some pretty good—" He stopped, his gaze landing on

Robyn. Apparently, he didn't trust her either, and Flash always saw the best in everyone. I suddenly found myself questioning my own judgment of character. Maybe she wasn't as good a woman as I wanted to believe.

"Some pretty good questions," he finished, turning back to me. "Sheriff Potts asked lots of them. Oodles and oodles. I'm impressed with her work ethic. She'll leave no stone unturned until she finds out who did this to Grandpa."

I had been about to cut Flash off—he never did know when to stop himself, especially when lying, and the longer he was allowed to continue, the larger and more unbelievable the lie became. But I forgot to, startled at the ease with which Flash referred to Keith as his grandfather. Someone he hadn't even met. The first time Flash had seen my father was when he'd stumbled into the aisle of the church, screaming like a lunatic.

"Those excellent questions the sheriff asked you," Robyn said, either not noticing the change in Flash's demeanor or pretending she hadn't. "They scare me. I'm worried about when it's my turn to be alone with her." She looked at me. "You say the people in your town are quick to judge, and I'm assuming your sheriff isn't any different. Would you describe her as more of an Andy Griffith or a Barney Fife?"

I smiled at her assumption that our town was akin to Mayberry from the *Andy Griffith Show*. I supposed in many ways, it was.

"Sheriff Potts can be stern, but she's fair," I said. "And because she's relatively new to Amor—only been here a few years—she doesn't have the same habits that most of the people around here have. You'll be fine."

"I don't know," Robyn said, not sounding convinced. "She didn't look like she thought much of me earlier."

I had noticed it too, and I was still a bit perplexed by that. It was very unlike Danielle.

Before I could think of a response, Sheriff Potts returned with Zoe, our newly appointed mayor. "You all should be heading home," the sheriff said. "Get something to eat—it's nearly one o'clock already." And then she and the mayor disappeared into the back room, the door shutting behind them.

"That's our cue to disappear," I said to Benji. "Want to meet me back at the house for a family meeting?" I lowered my voice and glanced at Flash and Lilly. "It worries me how happy the kids are. It makes me think they're up to something." I tugged on my dress—it was so constricting.

"You okay?" Lilly asked.

"I need to change my clothes. If I'm in this dress any longer, I'm afraid I'm going to accidentally destroy it, and it needs to be good for at least one more wearing."

Benji looked like he wanted to make a remark about how he could help me take it off, but then he remembered Robyn and the kids and stopped himself. "Good idea," was all he said, and then smiled.

"Ew, gross," Flash said. "Go on your honeymoon already."

Apparently, it hadn't fooled anyone.

"Maybe we should," I said, turning to Benji. "I know our marriage isn't official, but I made it down the aisle, and that has to count for something. Besides, we have reservations."

Benji's devious smile turned sad, which told me he wished we could, but we couldn't just run off, leaving my mom and Robyn to deal with things on their own.

"You're right," I said before he said anything, then glanced at Robyn. "I understand why you don't want to stay with us, but can I at least give you my number in case you need anything?"

She agreed, and we exchanged numbers, and then we walked toward the chapel—it was the only way to leave the church.

Which meant that I had to join the crowd of wedding guests, all impatiently waiting to escape through the front doors, and I was still in my wedding dress.

Even though none of this was my fault, I had never felt more embarrassed.

"Thank you all for coming," I said, smiling and giving them all a little wave as they shuffled outside. No one smiled back.

Benji's parents rushed up to him, having gotten stuck at the back of the crowd.

"The sheriff says we need to all come by the station at

Town Hall," Benji's dad said, casting anxious glances around the room. "She doesn't suspect your mom and me of anything, does she?"

"I saw her eyeing us," his mom said. "Of course she suspects us. Before we go, though, I'm hungry. Will there still be a reception? We haven't eaten lunch, and I was looking forward to those little sandwiches you were telling us about."

Benji tried to reassure his parents that they didn't need to worry about the sheriff arresting them, it was routine procedure, and, even though there wouldn't be a reception, they could have all the sandwiches they wanted, but they still seemed skeptical.

"Ooh, I want sandwiches too," Lilly said.

"I call dibs on the chicken salad croissants," Flash said. "Those are my favorite."

Tears pricked at my eyes. It was a silly thing to make me cry, but just that morning, I had been telling Flash that he was limited to two sandwiches and one piece of cake. We were supposed to be feeding the entire town, and I had been worried that we'd run out.

Now no one was celebrating, and we had more food than we knew what to do with.

I kept my kids moving toward the door as they argued about the rules of calling dibs, and I blinked away the moisture.

Most people avoided direct eye contact with us as we walked with them, likely feeling awkward about the whole debacle and not knowing what to say. That was just as well because, knowing Flash, he'd get bored of talking about sandwiches, and if we stopped long enough to talk to anyone, he'd manage to accuse half of our wedding guests of murder before making it outside.

He was good at that.

Unfortunately, my mom beat him to it.

5

M y mom was waiting for us in the doorway of the church, a pencil and scrap piece of paper in hand. "There you are," she said as we approached her. "I've been studying everyone and looking for people who seem nervous. Now it's quite a lengthy list, but I'm sure we can get this narrowed down. We'll want to start with Bob Larcher. He's been a nervous wreck since this whole thing started."

My mom hadn't bothered to lower her voice, and sound carried well enough that everyone, both inside and outside the church, could likely hear her.

It turned out that Bob and his girlfriend, Debbie, were standing right next to us in the crowd, my mom blocking their way out—I don't think she even realized it.

"Those are insane and wild accusations," he said, his arm around Debbie's shoulders. He pulled her in close. It had shocked everyone in town when Bob and Debbie had begun dating a few months earlier. They were polar opposites—her with her hair salon and pink highlights, and him working in HR at Town Hall. He was as straight an arrow as they came and not a prime candidate for a murder suspect.

"Of course I'm nervous—everyone should be nervous," Bob continued. "A man just died, and the sheriff wants to question the entire town." He glanced behind him, his gaze shifty, as if making sure Danielle hadn't heard. "I'm against it, by the way," he said, the volume of his voice lowering. "The questioning. We didn't even know the guy who died."

"Some people did," my mom countered. "Karla Simmons worked with him, and was fired because of him." She looked around the room. "Where is she anyway? I know she came to the wedding. It wouldn't have looked right if she hadn't."

"She ran out of the church as soon as that guy collapsed in the aisle," CJ said from behind us. "I'm trying to do the same, but you people keep blocking the exit." He owned our town's only auto repair shop, and he still had oil smudges on his forehead that he'd forgotten to clean. The man was nearly seventy years old, and I didn't think he'd be retiring anytime soon—he looked closer to fifty and had the energy to match.

My mom's eyes narrowed. "*That guy* was Keith Lawson, and he was Maddie's father. Show some respect."

My mom sticking up for my dad—that was a first.

CJ held up two hands. "Sorry, didn't mean to offend."

"Guilty conscience," my mom murmured, finally moving out of the doorway and onto the walkway that led to the parking lot. Wedding guests surged past her as she waved a piece of paper at me—the one where she'd written the names of half the town as murder suspects. She didn't seem to care whether they saw whose names she'd written on it. "We're having a family meeting at your place."

Even though I'd suggested the same thing to Benji a few minutes earlier, that had been before my mom had invited herself over. There was only so much I could handle right now, and apparently my mom's presence was the straw that would break my back.

I immediately protested while throwing anxious glances at our neighbors and friends. "Mom, it's been a trying day. I'm exhausted and—"

She cut me off. "No excuses. I'm sorry your wedding day wasn't what it should have been, but we have a lot to discuss. This murderer—they messed with the wrong family. And it's our job to make sure they know it."

I paused and looked over the parking lot. "Trish drove me over earlier," I said, unable to find her car in front of the church. "Have you seen her?"

"She was looking for you earlier," my mom said, suddenly very interested in her fingernails. "I told her we had everything under control here, and I sent her home."

Of course she had.

My mom and Trish had had a tumultuous relationship ever since I moved back to Amor with my kids after the divorce. I'd thought things would get better between the two—my mom's jealousy being the driving force—but it hadn't mattered how long Trish lived with me and the kids; my mom always treated Trish as if she were a stranger.

"I wish you wouldn't have done that, Mom. Now how am I supposed to get home?"

Benji gave me a wounded look. "You don't want to ride with me?"

I laughed and gave a pointed look at his small work truck. "I'm in a wedding dress. It will take up your entire cab, not to mention I doubt you keep that thing clean."

Lilly looked at me in horror. "You're not getting into his truck or any other car in your wedding dress. Why are you even still wearing that? Didn't you bring a change of clothes for after the wedding? You know, for when Benji whisked you away for your honeymoon?"

Right. I was supposed to do that, wasn't I. But then my mom had been freaking out about Cameron being at the church, and I'd been running late, and I'd thought I was doing pretty well when I managed to not forget my wedding dress.

Cameron.

Just like I'd forgotten my packed suitcase that was still sitting in the entryway by the front door, I'd forgotten that my ex-husband was still in town. I wondered where he'd gotten himself off to. Hopefully he wasn't causing too much trouble.

Lilly released a long sigh, accompanied by a giant eye roll, when she realized I had forgotten my getaway bag. "Well, you changed into your wedding dress at the church," she said. "That means you still have clothes here."

Right. My pajamas and slip-on sandals. It looked like I was going home from my wedding the same way I'd arrived at it—in flannel.

"I'll go change," I told them, then turned to Benji. "Mind running the kids and my mom home and then coming back for me?"

"I'd be happy to," he said, pulling me in for a quick kiss. There was concern in his eyes. He was worried about me, and I loved him for it.

But I was fine. I was used to life throwing curveballs, and even though this was a bigger one than I usually had to deal with, I had my family. In times like this, that was all I needed.

I looked past him, eyeing the bench seat in his truck. "Will all four of you fit?"

My mom looked at me like I was crazy. "I drove myself, dear. What did you think, that I walked all the way across town in this gorgeous dress? I don't think so." She glanced at the kids. "Come on, I'll take you home. Benji can wait for your mom, and then we'll have this much-needed family meeting." She glanced my way, her eyes daring me to say otherwise.

I stayed quiet.

"Sorry, Grandma. Benji was already counting on us driving with him. I don't want to hurt his feelings," Lilly said, then jumped into the cab of Benji's truck.

Flash jumped in after her. "I'm coming too."

My mom placed a hand on her hip. "No one wants to ride with me?" Her lips dipped into a frown. "I suppose now that your mom has Benji, I'm old news."

"Of course not, Grandma," Lilly said, then gave me a pleading look. Because what my children weren't telling her was that she was a terrible driver, and maybe they hadn't realized it when they were younger, but they were now very much afraid of getting in a car with her.

"They like the truck, that's all, Mom," I said. "You'll all be reunited in five minutes, and then after Benji picks me up, we'll get to the bottom of things, huh?"

Agreeing to a family meeting felt like the olive branch that my mom needed.

If only it were that simple.

I waved goodbye and re-entered the church. Mayor Flores...Zoe...was just leaving. It wasn't easy to squeeze past her—my dress took up most of the aisle, but I found that if I gathered enough material in my arms and hugged the dress as tight as I could, it was easier.

Even though we didn't speak as we passed each other, the pity in Zoe's eyes said everything she was thinking, and I hurried away and up the aisle.

When I arrived at the back room where I'd left my

things, I reached for the doorknob, but I stopped when it began to turn on its own. Instinctively, I stepped away from the door just as it flung open.

A man walked through, his steps quick, followed by the sheriff.

"Cameron," I said, a flood of emotions rolling over me. This was the first time I'd seen my ex-husband in a year.

He looked good, but also like he'd tried too hard. His clothes had been pressed to the point that they looked stiff, his hair gelled enough that I could balance a plate on his head.

I studied him. Underneath the handsome facade, he looked sad, and despite our rough past, I couldn't help but be worried for him.

"Maddie," he said with a slight nod. "Congratulations on your marriage. From what the kids tell me, Benji seems like a great guy."

I shifted uncomfortably in my wedding dress, wanting nothing more than to tear it off. At this point it was just a painful reminder of what had occurred—and what hadn't.

"There's nothing to congratulate me for," I said. "Never made it to the 'I dos.'" I paused, my tone softening. "All the same, thank you for coming. I know it meant a lot to the kids."

Sheriff Potts looked uncomfortable at being trapped with the two of us, so she excused herself and said, "I'll be in touch, Mr. Swallows."

I started at that, my gaze snapping to her. "You're not

actually thinking of him as a suspect, are you? Cameron never met my father."

Danielle refused to meet my gaze as she turned away. "Routine questions," she mumbled.

I looked at Cameron, who had no trouble making eye contact and keeping it. But there was some defiance to it, like I had no right to tell him who he could, and couldn't, interact with.

"What's going on between you two?" I asked. A sudden, and horrifying, thought occurred to me. "You two aren't... I mean..." I needed to warn the sheriff about getting involved romantically with Cameron—it wouldn't end well —but the words stuck in my throat. The very idea of it made me sick.

Cameron barked out a single laugh. "Relax, Maddie. Nothing is happening between the sheriff and me. Although—" He gave the sheriff an appraising look.

Danielle's eyes narrowed. "Not a chance."

He raised a shoulder. "A guy can try."

"If you must know," she said, releasing a hard breath, looking like she was about to deliver some very painful news. "Your ex-husband—Mr. Swallows—has offered his expertise in helping solve this unfortunate, and difficult, case. And I've accepted."

6

I spun to face Cameron. "Is this a joke? Why would you offer to help with a situation you know nothing about? I invited you to the wedding because the kids wanted you here, and I appreciate you coming. But your duty is done. I'm sure you have a book signing or a talk show you need to be getting to."

Cameron straightened. "There's nowhere else I'd rather be than here. In fact, before coming down, I'd already decided to take the whole week off work. Thought that while you and Benji were on your honeymoon, the kids and I could spend some time together. They'll be moving away soon, you know."

Yes, I did know. Frankly, I was surprised that Cameron had even remembered, or that he was willing to take a week off work. He never took time off, not even for a vacation, let alone to spend time with his kids. I hoped there wasn't an ulterior motive, though what it would be, I had no idea.

"So, why not actually do that while you're here?" I asked. "Spend time with them. No need to get yourself involved in local affairs."

I guessed that was what I was calling murder investigations now. Local affairs.

Cameron was quiet for a moment before he shrugged. "Helping solve a murder wasn't exactly what I had in mind when I came to Amor, but why not? From what the sheriff has been telling me, solving murders is what our kids like to do best."

Unfortunately, that was true, but I hadn't wanted Cameron to know it. I'd gone to great lengths over the years to keep him from finding out.

His eyes softened. "I can help—you know I can."

I felt myself giving in, and I steeled myself against it. Today had been bad enough—dealing with him was the last thing I needed right now. "The psychology of serial killers is your expertise, and that is not what this is," I said. "Besides, you know nothing about this town and the people in it. Nothing about my father. You've never worked with Sheriff Potts before—"

"I'd like his help," Danielle interrupted.

I'd thought my wedding day couldn't get any worse, but having my ex-husband sticking around, investigating the death of my father? I didn't think I could handle that.

"You don't need him," I said to Danielle. "You're the

best sheriff our town has ever had, and you haven't even had time to investigate. Better yet, let me help. How many times have we worked together in the past, and how many times have I been able to see things that others have missed?"

Danielle nodded thoughtfully, but her expression—it was one of guilt. She'd already made up her mind.

"He's in and I'm out," I said with resignation.

"I'm sorry, Maddie. I know it hasn't always seemed like I've appreciated you," she said. "Of course, that's mostly due to your family walking a very thin line between what's legal and—well, I know when it comes to your kids, it's better not to ask too many questions. But working with an expert in the field—I can't turn that down."

I supposed I understood. Cameron was the one who had written multiple books on the subject. He'd been on TV. Even been asked to serve as an expert witness in high-profile cases. How could the sheriff not accept his help?

Me? Sure, I had a PhD. I'd worked at the same university as Cameron, but I had never done more than teach psychology to undergrads. And now I ran a small-town therapy office.

What could I possibly contribute that Cameron couldn't—other than the burning desire to bring justice to whoever had killed my father?

Maybe the sheriff didn't think she needed my help. Maybe, like my mom, I was old news. But I could certainly be just as much help as Cameron. More, even.

I had the motivation.

And I was going to prove it.

"WE'RE HOME," I said, walking into the house and tossing my dress bag onto the couch. It felt good to be back in my flannels again.

My mom walked in, and her gaze immediately landed on the wedding dress. "Really, Maddie, you need to take better care of your things. You'll need that dress again for when you finally get married, and who knows, maybe in a few years Lilly will want to wear it to her own wedding."

"No, I won't," Lilly called from the other room. "It's not my style. Besides, it's cursed now that Grandpa was murdered while Mom was wearing it. She didn't even manage to make it through the ceremony. We should probably burn it."

Awesome. So glad that during this time of tragedy, my family was being their usual, supportive selves.

"Good thing she didn't get married in her pajamas," Benji said, tossing me a teasing smile. "I don't think she could give those up, cursed or not."

I stuck my tongue out at him, then glanced at my mom. "How are you doing? You know, with...everything."

It had been chaos all day, and I hadn't had the chance to check in with my mom. Maybe she hadn't liked my dad —hated him even. But they had loved each other at one point in their lives, and to watch him die like that—that had to be traumatizing.

My mom refused to look at me as she picked up the dress bag. "I'm fine. Why wouldn't I be?" She busied herself hanging the dress on the front window's curtain rod, then began straightening the pillows on the couch. "You know, other than all my hard work going to waste. We won't get a refund from the caterer, by the way. I asked her to deliver all the food to the house, so we're going to be eating chicken salad sandwiches for quite a while. We'll also have plenty of fruit and cake. Good thing Flash doesn't leave for his new job for a few weeks—we'll need his help to eat through all of it."

I watched her for a moment, not saying anything. I could tell she was fighting unwanted emotions, and as much as I didn't want to make her uncomfortable, it wasn't healthy to pretend that my dad's death hadn't affected her.

"It's okay to be sad," I said. "Even if you didn't like him, it's okay to cry."

My mom whipped to me, anger flashing in her eyes. Maybe I'd misread the situation. "It's not okay, Maddie. Because all those years ago, I did love him. For all his faults, I never gave up on him." Her voice hitched. "He did, though. He gave up. And then, when he finally put his life back together, he chose someone else. Someone that wasn't me. That's not okay. I don't want to be sad that he's gone."

And then she slumped onto the couch—onto those pillows she'd just rearranged—and sobbed.

Benji stepped forward, looking concerned, but I waved him away. I'd never seen my mom cry like this before. I'd seen her angry plenty of times, but rarely sad.

He gave a hesitant nod, squeezed my hand, and then disappeared into the kitchen, giving me and my mom the space we needed.

I approached her cautiously. "He wasn't rejecting you, Mom. Do you know why he never showed up—not until today?"

She glanced at me but remained quiet.

"Because he knew he didn't deserve you," I said, sitting next to her. "He knew what he'd done. He knew how much he'd hurt us. That's why he brought Robyn with him. Because he couldn't bear to face us alone." I rested my hand on hers. "It took a lot of courage for him to show up today. And it isn't fair that he was so cruelly taken. It's our job to find the closure we need—the closure we deserve. No one else is going to do that for us."

My mom glanced up at me, her eyes filled with moisture. "The sheriff thinks I did it. She thinks I hated him, and I can understand why. But I would never have killed him."

"Of course you wouldn't," I said. "Under all that anger, you still loved him." I patted her hand and stood. "And we have to prove it before Cameron convinces the sheriff otherwise."

My mom's gaze snapped to me. "What does he have to do with any of this?"

I stayed quiet as I gathered my thoughts, trying to figure out how to explain the situation. I didn't like talking negatively about him when the kids were around, and I never knew when they were listening in. They had a bad habit of eavesdropping.

"Cameron has convinced the sheriff that he's an expert in these kinds of matters and that he can help her solve this murder," I finally said.

"Why would she ever agree to such a thing?" my mom spluttered, pushing herself off the couch. "He doesn't know this town, and he never met Keith. It's strange that he'd even volunteer for something like this. Doesn't he have a job he has to get back to?"

I gave her a weak smile, because that had been my argument when speaking to the sheriff, almost word for word. "He said he took a week off work to spend time with the kids while Benji and I went on our honeymoon. Now he wants to spend that time playing detective. Said that the kids would enjoy helping him solve it."

My mom gave an aggressive shake of her head. "He's searching for an unfulfilled fantasy. Sure, Cameron has studied serial killers—interviewed them behind bars—but he's never met a murderer in the wild. It's a thrill-seeking thing for him. And he's going to put Flash and Lilly in danger while doing it."

I stiffened, her words rubbing me the wrong way. My

first instinct was to check to make sure the kids weren't in earshot. My second instinct was to stick up for Cameron. To tell her that it was unfair for her to make those kinds of assertions.

But this wasn't an issue of fairness—it was an issue of truth.

I thought back to all those family dinner conversations when we'd been married. Cameron had loved talking about his work—almost seemed giddy about it. I'd hated it.

"Who's the psychologist now?" I said, trying to keep my tone light.

Her lips dipped, and I knew I hadn't succeeded.

"Are you saying I'm wrong?" she asked.

I hesitated.

"You know I'm not," she said when I didn't answer right away. "And what concerns me most is that Cameron will have no qualms accepting the easiest answers—true or not —even if that means pinning Keith's murder on me. Because I'm not blind. I'm the easiest answer. Then he'll pat himself on the back for a job well done and go on his merry way. Wouldn't lose a single night's sleep over it."

"I doubt it will come to that," I quickly said, though the way things had gone in our lives recently, I couldn't rule anything out. "Besides, if Cameron is only helping the sheriff for the thrill of it, he'll quickly learn that investigating murders isn't all that exciting. It's a lot of asking questions of perfectly normal people. He'll get bored."

"And if he doesn't?"

"Then we need to figure out who murdered Keith before Cameron has time to make any wild accusations."

"Mom," Lilly called from the top of the stairs. We turned as she thundered down the steps. She arrived in the front room, breathless. "Dad is on the phone with Flash right now. He wants our help investigating Grandpa's murder, and he's acting super weird about it. Like, he's asking Flash how good his hacking skills are and what kind of stuff we've done for you in the past. It feels like he's trying to gauge how far we're willing to go. I don't know why, but...it feels wrong."

I looked at my mom with alarm. "I have to stop this."

And then I ran upstairs.

I had an ex-husband to get rid of.

7

I held my hand out for Flash's phone. "I need to talk to your father."

"But Mom, he wants to help," he protested, glancing up from his computer. He had his phone on the desk, the speaker icon lit as he typed on the computer. "Dad has a lot of experience with this stuff."

"And I don't?"

Cameron's voice filled the room. "You're a therapist, Maddie. And you do a lot of good for your patients. But you don't have the same background that I do, and frankly, I'm not sure your small-town sheriff is cut out for these types of investigations either. Why is it so hard for you to admit that I'm the expert here? Let me do what I'm good at."

I bit my tongue, wanting to tell him he was wrong. That I had plenty of experience dealing with murderers, and I was actually quite good at catching them. I only wished I found myself in these situations a little less often.

"I thought the same as you about our sheriff," I said. "But she started in the big city before moving here, and she knows what she's doing. You can trust her to do her job."

Silence.

"Why won't you let me do this for you?" he finally asked. "I know I've made a lot of mistakes in the past, but the victim—this is your father we're talking about. Let me help you find justice. You deserve that much."

Meaning that Cameron didn't think I could handle it on my own. He thought I needed saving, even though I was the one who'd been doing the saving for the past four years. And for what I couldn't do on my own, I relied on the people who actually cared about me.

Benji. Lilly. Flash. My mom. My town.

I'd rely on any of them before I'd ever come to my ex-husband for help.

"I don't need you, Cameron. Either spend time with your kids or go home. But leave this investigation alone."

And then I punched the red icon to end the call.

"Mom," Flash protested. "That was my conversation with Dad. You had no right to do that."

"And he had no right to insert himself into our business."

Flash spun in his chair so he faced me. "You insert yourself in people's business all the time. So does

Grandma. Why do you think the sheriff is always frustrated with you?"

I stilled. Flash never spoke to me like this.

His dad's bad attitude was rubbing off on him.

Or there was the remote possibility that Flash was right. I hated to admit it, because I still didn't want Cameron anywhere near me, the sheriff, or this investigation, but maybe I was letting my personal feelings about Cameron get in the way of the bigger picture. I couldn't deny that he did have experience with the psychology of murderers.

"Okay," I relented. "We can include your dad, when necessary. But he doesn't have to be involved in every step of the investigation. He's more like a consultant." I leaned down and looked at Flash's computer. "What were you two working on?"

Flash studied me for a moment before turning back to his computer. "We need to know everyone who lived in Amor at the time that Grandpa left. Dad asked me to pull tax records for current residents and cross-match them with those who were paying taxes at the time of your birth."

I had to give it to Cameron, he worked fast. I'd only managed to get out of my wedding dress, and he'd already had Flash pulling up tax records. I tried not to think about the legal ramifications of what they were doing—the damage had been done, and there was nothing I could do about it now.

"What have you found?" I asked.

Flash leaned back in his chair and ran a hand through his hair. "That nobody moves out of this town. They stay here until they die."

There was a lot of truth to that.

"Well, dead people don't pay taxes."

Flash nodded to the screen. "I limited it to anyone who is over the age of sixty, because they would have been around twenty years old when Grandpa left. There are two-hundred and eleven names."

"That's too many," I said. "Can you print this list off? We can show it to your grandma and see if any of the names stand out to her."

Flash scrunched his nose. "Do people still use printers? I'd rather send the file to her phone."

"Your Grandma isn't going to look through two hundred names on a tiny screen," I said. "She's going to want to sit down at the kitchen table with a highlighter."

Flash tried to hold back a groan, but a small one still managed to escape. "Fine. I do have an old printer and extra ink that I only use for emergencies. I suppose I can dig out some computer paper."

Ten minutes later, I was holding a list of two hundred and eleven names, and none of them meant anything to me.

"Mom," I called when I got downstairs. "I have a puzzle for you."

Benji walked in from the living room. "She left a couple

minutes ago. She said to tell you she was heading home for the afternoon and she'd be back for dinner. She requested lasagna."

Of course she had. Only my mother would request I make dinner on my wedding day, when I was supposed to be on my honeymoon.

Benji placed a hand on my arm. "She didn't look good, Maddie. Looked like she was having some sort of breakdown."

I had been so busy trying to push down my own emotions, I'd forgotten my mom was doing the same.

But how much worse was it for her? She had loved my dad. Married him. Had a daughter with him. For me, he'd only been someone we didn't talk about. A subject that wasn't worth mentioning.

I glanced down at the list of names in my hands and knew I couldn't do this to her—at least not right now.

She needed a daughter. Not a detective.

"I'll go check on her," I said.

Benji held my arm, preventing me from leaving. I avoided his gaze when he asked, "How are you doing?"

"I'll be doing a lot better once we find my father's murderer."

His gaze didn't waver. "Today has been horrible for your family. Traumatic. I understand your need to find who did this. But if one of your patients had a day like today, what would you tell them?"

I hated when people did that to me—turned the tables

and made me ask the hard questions. I was a lot better at giving advice than I was at taking it.

Especially when it came to taking my own advice.

"I would tell them they deserved a month off from life," I conceded. "I'd say they needed to be kind to themselves. That they needed time to grieve. They needed space."

Benji nodded. "And what would you tell them if they told you they were investigating their father's murder within hours of it happening?"

I didn't like these questions, and I didn't answer right away, but Benji wouldn't let me go with that gaze of his.

"That they needed to leave it to the professionals—that taking that kind of burden upon themselves wasn't healthy and they needed to take a step back from it all."

Benji fell silent and raised an eyebrow, letting me sit with all the advice I'd just given my hypothetical patient.

"You want me to just pretend all this never happened?" I finally asked. "Pretend my ex-husband isn't investigating the death of my father and dragging my kids into it? Pretend that people don't think my mother killed him? I'm supposed to stand by and watch her fall apart, while taking time for myself?"

Benji's lips parted. "I didn't realize Cameron was still in town."

"Yes. And he's convinced Sheriff Potts that he's the best man to help her with the investigation—that his expertise is exactly what she needs."

Benji took my hands in his. "Look, I know you've never

been one to stand by and do nothing. That's one of the things I love most about you. But like you told your fictional patient—you need time to grieve. Maybe this is one time when you shouldn't be involved."

I pulled my hands from Benji's. "You're right, of course. But it's because of Cameron's involvement that I need to be. I don't trust him or his intentions. He's going to be throwing accusations right and left without knowing the people behind them, and I'll be left cleaning up his mess."

"You want to find the murderer before he does," Benji said, his voice quiet.

I nodded. "Yes. Otherwise, it could be my mom he sets his sights on, and the sheriff will listen to him. She respects his opinion. I can't let that happen."

"You're sure this isn't just about proving something to Cameron?" Benji said, folding his arms across his chest, his expression skeptical.

Okay, maybe there was a little part of me that felt like I had something to prove—that wanted Cameron to finally realize what he'd missed out on. Someone who was intelligent and beautiful, and who could hold her own.

Basically, this was my version of Princess Diana's revenge dress, and I recognized it wasn't exactly healthy.

"Does it really matter?" I said, avoiding Benji's gaze. "We have a murderer to catch and a wedding ceremony to finish. And it has to be done in that order."

8

I knew it was stupid—I had nothing to prove to Cameron. We'd been divorced for four years. Sure, he had the career that had brought him fame and prestige. But I had my own business. I had my family. And I had found love.

It was Cameron I felt sorry for. Once he got bored of Amor, he'd disappear for another year, self-absorbed, never thinking again of his children until I called to remind him of their birthdays or to make sure their Christmas presents were in the mail.

And yet, every time Cameron and I talked, I felt the need to prove I was okay. That my life was better without him in it. It was a knee-jerk reaction that I didn't know how to control.

I'd long since stopped trying to fight it. So I grabbed my purse.

I was going to first check on my mother, and then I had
a murder to solve.

"What are you doing?" Benji asked. I wondered if my
face had betrayed everything I'd been thinking. It usually
did.

"I told you, I'm going to check on my mother."

Benji looked like he didn't quite believe me.

Flash thundered down the stairs. "I'm coming too. I'll
call Dad and tell him to meet us there."

I turned on my son. "No. Absolutely not. We're just
stopping by to make sure she's okay, and your dad's presence isn't going to be helpful with that."

Confusion pulled at Flash's eyebrows. "But we need to
find who killed Grandpa. That's what will help Grandma
feel better, and Dad is our best chance at that."

I forced myself to take a long breath. My kids had first
gotten involved with murder investigations because they'd
wanted to spend more time with me. At least, that was the
reason they'd given me. I was pretty sure the real reason
was that they had a morbid curiosity that compelled them
to be involved with things they shouldn't.

Regardless, it had become a sort of family activity—
one commonality we all shared. Now Flash was trying to
do the same thing with his dad—get him to spend time
with him.

"Your grandma needs to take it easy right now," I said,
my tone softer. "But you can invite your dad over to our
house later this afternoon. How about we pick up some ice

cream on our way home? Your dad always loved a good bowl of rocky road."

"Ice cream sounds good," said Flash. "We'll need it to help us come up with ideas about who our prime suspects are."

I had meant that Cameron could join us for ice cream —and ice cream only. The less we discussed the investigation with him, the better. But Flash looked so happy at the new plan, I hated to be the one to squash it.

"When you invite your dad," I told Flash, "you need to make sure he knows I'm the one calling the shots with anything related to your grandpa's death. Your dad will be here as an observer only."

Flash pulled out his phone. "What if he has really good ideas?"

Lilly walked into the room, her camera bag slung over one shoulder. "Dad won't give Mom a chance to express her ideas if we let him. She should control the conversation but can ask him for his thoughts when she's feeling ready for them."

Lilly, always my champion.

And then I noticed Benji standing to the side of the room, looking like he didn't know if he was coming or going.

"When the kids and I get back from my mom's—" I said, approaching him.

His gaze dropped, and he finished my thought for me. "You don't know if it would be a good idea if I'm here.

Fiancé in the same room as the ex-husband and all that. Plus, six is a crowd. I get it."

"Six?"

"Yeah, you, the kids, Cameron, and your mom. I would make six."

I started to protest. "I was going to say that when we get back, I'll have a tub of mint chocolate chip with your name on it. You don't need to leave just because Cameron will be here. I am marrying you, and he's going to have to learn to deal with it. As far as my mom goes—"

"You know your mom will get involved in whatever you are plotting, even if you try to keep her out of it. It's a family matter. A family I'm not a part of yet. Technically."

It sounded so sad when Benji said it. And it wasn't true.

Because I really did want Benji there, and despite him thinking that I needed to leave things alone this time, I could tell he wanted to be there as well. With or without the marriage certificate, he had been a part of this family for a long time now. He didn't deserve to be left out.

And yet, Cameron's presence complicated things.

"I'm sorry," I said. "I would rather Cameron not be here at all, but the kids are so desperate to spend time with their dad, no matter the form it takes, and—"

"I said that I get it," Benji said, interrupting me. "That doesn't mean I have to like it." And then he turned and went up the stairs.

This day was getting further and further from what it was supposed to be.

. . .

I HAD PLANNED on driving to my mom's, but Benji had parked behind my car in the driveway and, considering the way we'd left things, I didn't want to ask him to move it. So the kids and I decided to walk.

Lilly held us up by stopping to take a picture every other minute, apparently forgetting what our true mission was.

"How can you still have anything left to take pictures of?" Flash asked. "I swear you've photographed every square inch of this town."

Lilly glanced up from her camera. "Even if I took a picture of the same flower every day for a year, I'd have three hundred and sixty-five different photos. Every day, the lighting is just a bit different or the flower is facing a new direction or the background has changed. You'd notice if you weren't on your computer all the time."

"My computer is how I'm moving away at the age of seventeen and have a job that other hackers could only dream of."

Lilly shook her head. "I can't believe people are actually going to pay you to break into computer systems. There's something wrong about that."

"Just like I can't believe people get paid to hold a camera," Flash retorted.

Flash and Lilly had often argued in the past, but it had increased lately. I was pretty sure it was because they were going to miss each other and they didn't want to admit it. We'd all gotten good at shoving down our feelings recently. I was a terrible example of it.

"And yet they do," Lilly said, then abruptly turned from the sidewalk and onto someone's yard. "Just one minute, Mom. There's an adorable lawn ornament I want to get a quick picture of." She lifted her camera.

As she tilted the camera, trying to find the best angle, an older gentleman burst through the front door with more speed than I thought possible—or wise—for a man of his age. "What are you doing, you thief," he shouted.

I didn't remember the gentleman's name, but I remembered seeing him at town meetings on occasion. From what I'd heard, he rarely ventured outside his home.

Lilly dropped the camera and opened her mouth to say something, but nothing came out, so I hurried over to help.

"Good afternoon. This is my daughter, Lilly, and she is no thief, I promise. We were just admiring your lawn ornament." I looked down to see what it was that had caught Lilly's eye. It was a garden gnome with a blue hat and yellow jacket. It was holding out a bouquet of mushrooms, as if they were flowers, and it had a mischievous grin. The gnome didn't seem to represent the old man's personality at all, but in my line of work, I'd discovered there was much more to a person beyond what we could see on the surface.

The man harrumphed. "Do you always use a camera to admire objects that aren't yours?"

Lilly nodded, gaining some courage now that I was there. "I do, yes. I find that I have a difficult time remembering the beautiful things I see, and I love being able to go back to them over and over again."

The man's expression softened. "I'm sorry. Someone has been stealing my gnomes—they were my wife's gnomes. And I thought... Well, anyway, take all the pictures you want."

"That's terrible," I said. "Do you have any idea who might be doing it?"

He shook his head sadly. "No, but always in broad daylight. My gnomes are there in the morning when I come out for the daily paper, and then gone when I come out for the mail. Most have been returned after a few days —as if the culprits got in trouble with their mothers and were forced to return them. And yet, the pattern continues, the same gnomes being repeatedly stolen."

I gave him a sympathetic smile and extended my hand. "I'm Maddie Swallows. My family lives one street over."

The man stiffened, and as quickly as he'd forgiven us for trespassing, his sadness turned to anger. "I know you who are. You're Laurie Lawson's daughter. I changed my mind. No pictures. No camera. And I never want to see you on my property again."

And then he turned away and hobbled back inside.

Lilly and I shared bewildered looks and walked back to where Flash was waiting for us on the sidewalk.

"We could have used you for moral support," Lilly said. "What were you doing, hiding back here?"

Flash threw an anxious glance at the house. "Sorry. It's just..." He lowered his voice. "Old people make me nervous."

Lilly laughed. "Does Grandma make you nervous?"

Flash shook his head as we resumed walking. "No, but she's not that old. That guy—he's like one of those sea turtles that have lived hundreds of years. Or Yoda. They may be slow, but they have some fight left in them."

"So, you're afraid he can beat you up?" Lilly asked.

I also found the thought hilarious, considering that Flash was taller than I was—he had surpassed me a couple of years ago, and I still wasn't used to it.

Flash gave a solemn nod. "It's more than that. When you get to that age, you can do Jedi mind tricks and snap people in half just by thinking it."

I was going to miss Flash so much when he was gone— he saw the world in such an interesting way. As much as I loved Benji, I was afraid that once Lilly and Flash moved out, things would be, dare I say, boring.

That was another thought I had to bury deep. But despite my best efforts, all these thoughts were building up —I needed to talk to Trish. She could help me process them. Except, she was one of the issues I was hiding from. She'd tried to tell me that morning that she was planning on leaving town. It had been difficult when she'd moved out of the house a couple of weeks earlier, but I hadn't thought she'd leave Amor. What was I going to do without her?

Oh, dear. It was surfacing. I mentally squashed that down too.

We walked another block before arriving at my mother's house. When we entered, the scent of fresh bread enveloped us, and I was instantly concerned. Bread was my mom's coping mechanism. When I had been anxious about Benji and my upcoming wedding, I'd compulsively cooked and cleaned and kept myself busy. I should have realized where I'd gotten that tendency from, because for my mom, it was bread. And if we didn't help her out of her funk soon, she would make enough bread to feed the entire town, and maybe the next town over.

"Mom," I called. "The kids and I came by to visit."

My mom poked her head out of the kitchen. She was wearing an apron, and flour was streaked along her face and through her hair. I wasn't surprised to see that she was also wearing her green chile earrings. She'd always said they were her comfort earrings—the ones she wore when she was sad.

"You never visit unannounced. It's always me who visits you," she said as she took in the three of us. "And why are you still in your pajamas?"

I stifled a groan. "Forget about the pajamas, will you? They're comfy."

My mom studied us once more. "I'll forget about the pajamas if you'll tell me why you're really here and what that piece of paper is that Flash is holding."

My heart dropped. I hadn't realized he'd brought the list with him. My mom was too fragile for something like that—this had truly only been a welfare check. A visit to make sure she was okay. Asking her to identify potential murder suspects—it could push her over the edge.

"It's nothing," I said quickly. "Homework that Flash is doing, that's all."

Crap. Flash had graduated early—he didn't have homework anymore. I hoped she wouldn't notice.

My mom's eyes narrowed. "Flash didn't do homework even when he was in school."

That was true. He'd said it was too easy and he had better things to do with his time—like competing in hacking competitions.

My mom held out her hand. "Give it to me. If it has something to do with Keith's death, I want to know about it. And I want to help. Unless you'd rather I make more bread."

With a threat like that hanging over our heads, we had no choice but to give her the list. As soon as my mom saw it, she knew exactly what we needed her to do.

9

"These people," my mom said, sliding into a chair at the dining room table, highlighter in hand. "They're all my age or older."

Flash nodded. "We aren't looking for someone younger, because they would have either been too young to remember Grandpa or not yet born."

My mom's gaze snapped up at the casual way Flash had used the term "Grandpa." The kids had been using it all day, and I still wasn't used to it.

"I suppose he was your grandfather," she said, looking back at the paper. "Even if he didn't deserve it."

"Was he really that bad?" Lilly asked. "Mom says we aren't supposed to ask about him, but surely we can now that...you know."

"Now that we saw him die," my mom finished for her, and sighed. "Yes, I suppose you deserve that much. The thing is—I don't want to speak ill of the dead, but I also don't want you to think he was someone he wasn't."

She glanced at me, and I gave a little nod, indicating she should continue. In all honesty, I knew nearly nothing about my father, and I was interested in what she had to say as well.

"Your...grandfather..." she started, looking back at the kids, "was not a good man. Whatever changes he's made, if that woman is to be believed, are new."

"Robyn," Lilly interrupted.

My mom didn't look like she appreciated my stepmother's name being said in her house. "Yes. Her. Anyway, the day your grandfather left me and your mother was a good day. When I was pregnant, he spent more time drinking with his friends than he spent at home taking care of me. He would get in fights and come home with bruises or black eyes, but then lie and say that he ran into a table or something stupid like that. But I knew—if I had lit a match within a yard of him, he would have exploded into flames."

This part I had known. The alcoholic father who didn't care about anyone else, let alone us. The man we were better off without.

"And then your mother was born," my mom said, her lips dipping further. She looked like she was near tears. "I thought maybe things would be better now that we had our beautiful baby girl." She glanced at me. "She was perfect. A bit fussy, but some things never change, do they?"

I wanted to protest at that—but I needed to let her say whatever was needed, the good and the bad, however true or untrue. This was her story to tell, not mine.

My kids thought my mom's comment was hilarious, and they snickered.

"Focus on the part where she said I was perfect," I said with a slight smile.

"Grandpa didn't change when Mom was born, did he?" Lilly said, her voice soft as she turned her attention back to my mom.

My mom shook her head. "No. Things only got worse. He was fired for stealing—he had been the manager of a sporting goods store, but the more he drank, the more he either made mistakes or purposely fudged the numbers. I had to find a job, and a babysitter. I was practically a single mom before he left, so there was nothing but relief when he walked out that door."

"Grandpa left his family because he was fired from a job? That's a dumb reason," Flash said. He had a thoughtful expression, like he was trying to make sense of it all but was falling short. Lilly seemed more invested in the emotional aspect.

And me?

Like my mom, I would have been happy to never have to talk about it again. Avoidance was my specialty.

"I wish that had been the reason he left," my mom said. "Unfortunately, it was a lot worse than that." She pulled in a long breath. "Now that Keith didn't have a job and I was the one bringing in the money, he could do whatever he wanted all day without any real consequences. He was loving the unemployed lifestyle. No, what really did it was him sending a young man to the hospital." She paused long enough to wipe her eyes with her sleeve. "I had known about the fighting, despite what Keith claimed. Everyone in town made sure I knew and wanted to know what I planned to do about it. But what could I do, other than throw him out?"

"And you couldn't do that," Lilly said, leaning forward. "You had loved him enough to marry him. That doesn't just disappear, does it?"

My mom was silent for a moment, her head bent. I heard a sniffle.

"There were days I wasn't sure I loved him anymore," my mom said, her voice quiet. "Dreaded when he'd come home. And yet, I couldn't do it. Couldn't leave. So I suppose, yes, I did love him, in a tragic sort of way. But then he went and hit that young man so hard that he went into a coma. And the poor boy never came out of it. That's the real reason Keith left. Because if he didn't, the town was going to do it for him. The sheriff certainly didn't seem to want to be bothered. This town—it was a bit like the Wild West back then."

"I'm glad you stayed behind," I said. "That you didn't leave with him."

She glanced at me. "I wish I could say it was my choice. But he never asked me to come. One morning I woke up and he was gone. I hated myself for crying over it, but for all his faults, he never once hit me or hurt you. He could be kind. Gentle. A wonderful sense of humor. That's what I'd fallen in love with. So much so that when we'd been dating, I'd only seen the man I wanted him to be and ignored the red flags that indicated I should dig deeper."

I nodded at the list on the table in front of my mom. "Sounds like he wasn't exactly Mr. Popular around here. Is there someone on that list with reason to harbor a forty-year grudge?"

We were back to business, because I didn't want to hear any more about how my so-called father had hurt my mother. And I didn't want my kids calling him Grandpa. That was supposed to be a term of endearment, and my mom was right. He didn't deserve it.

It took my mom a moment to refocus on the list in front of her. "Truthfully, I might have to highlight them all."

"You should focus on the ones who hated him the most," Flash said. "Dad says a lot of murders are crimes of passion. I told him it made sense because we'd seen a lot of those. Remember the hot air balloon festival, Mom? Everyone thought it was—"

"You told your dad about the festival?" I interrupted, panic suddenly flooding my chest. I had wanted to keep that between us. If Cameron found out just how many murder investigations we had been a part of over the years...

I forced myself to breathe. When we'd first been divorced, I'd been afraid that if Cameron wanted custody of the kids, he could use that knowledge against me. That the court would see me as an unfit parent, letting my kids run around solving murders.

But they were older now. Legal age. No one could take them away from me.

"Sure," Flash said. "Dad thinks I was exaggerating, though. Might even think I made the whole thing up." His lips dipped into a frown at the thought of his dad not believing him.

I put on my best upbeat smile and changed the subject. "You and Lilly said you learned something while talking with the sheriff. What was it?"

Flash perked up at that, as did Lilly.

"Oh, yeah," he said, straightening in his chair. "This actually might help you, Grandma. It's not so much something we learned but something we saw."

Lilly jumped in, talking over her brother. "We saw Grandpa...Keith...in an argument outside the church just before the wedding."

Flash shot her a scowl before turning back to my mom and me. "Yeah, with CJ. His name's on the list. Did he have anything against Keith?"

My mom scrunched up her nose as she thought. "I can't remember anything specifically," she finally said. "But I wouldn't be surprised if he did. I think he'd just started working at the auto shop around that time."

"What did the sheriff say when you told her about the argument?" I asked.

Flash shrugged and looked at Lilly. "No idea. I wasn't paying attention."

Lilly sighed, like she didn't know what she was going to do with her brother. "She didn't say much, but she did seem very interested in it. Kept muttering something about dissolving rust."

My mouth formed a small O. I knew exactly what the sheriff was thinking.

"That's how the sheriff thinks Keith died," I said, my words slow. I didn't want to jump to conclusions, but if CJ had been arguing with Keith, and CJ had access to a substance that could have been the murder weapon, my mom needed to know.

"What is?" my mom asked me, her gaze intense.

"Oxalic acid poisoning. And it's found in things like anti-rust and cleaning products."

Lilly looked at me. "I wish we never would have said anything to the sheriff about it, but everything was so intense, you know? People were freaking out and trying to figure out what was happening. We were just trying to help."

"You don't think CJ really did it, do you?" Flash asked. "He's one of the nicest guys in town. Said if I want to learn how to change my own oil, he'd teach me, and if I like it well enough, he could teach me other things, and I could even work in his shop with him."

"But you'd hate everything about that," I said.

Flash grinned. "I know. It's the thought that counts." His smile dipped. "I suppose we need to highlight his name on the list, though. Gotta be fair to everyone. Your name too, Grandma."

She spluttered. "My name's on here?"

Lilly nodded. "Gotta be fair."

My mom scowled and looked at me. "I don't like the way you raised these kids."

"It's funny that you think I had anything to do with how they turned out—which is pretty darn great, by the way."

Flash and Lilly nodded in agreement, and then Flash looked at the paper in front of my mom.

"If you don't like being on the list, you better find more suspects. Because like we said, we're nothing but fair. And you're not in a great position right now, Grandma."

10

The kids and I returned home from my mom's house, exhausted. What I wouldn't have given to be in a secluded luxury resort with Benji right then, soaking in a hot tub while looking out at the mountains.

Benji had immediately recognized that I needed an hour to myself and, rather than the kids inviting Cameron over for rocky road, Benji had taken Flash and Lilly to the diner for ice cream.

I appreciated the gesture; however, instead of taking a much-needed nap like I'd intended, I lay in bed, staring at the ceiling because my mind wouldn't shut off.

I couldn't stop thinking about the time we'd spent with my mom.

After she'd finished telling the kids and me the tragic tales about my father, she had quickly highlighted several names on Flash's list, though she had still been grumpy that the kids were even considering her as a suspect.

Thankfully, she'd managed to highlight three people other than herself and CJ. One of them had died a month earlier, so that left only two other people. One was the elderly father of the man that Keith had put in a coma, and the other was Karla, the woman who had worked at the sporting goods store with him.

"Don't forget Robyn," my mom had said. "Add her to the list. Being married to that man taught me one thing, and that is anyone is capable of murder. If Keith hadn't left me, it wouldn't have been long before I snapped his neck."

The kids and I had both stared at her in horror.

"You can't say things like that," I'd said. "Especially not right now."

My mom had sniffed and looked away. "It's not like I would really have done it, even if I did have it all planned out. I had you to think of."

That was a small consolation.

My mom had then ordered us home so she could be alone.

MY EYES SNAPPED OPEN, as if I had been startled awake. I must have finally dozed off. I sat up and stretched my neck. It was stiff.

A knock on the front door.

"Benji," I called. "The door is unlocked."

Silence. And then a louder knock.

If it were actually Benji, my kids would have already burst into the house by now.

I tensed. It wasn't like I never had visitors, but usually the kind of visitors I got just after a murder weren't the type I wanted to deal with. My guess was that it was either Danielle or—well, my mom never knocked, so it had to be Danielle.

I pulled in a long breath as I walked downstairs, preparing myself for all the questions she would throw at me, and then I opened the door. Better to get it over with.

It was not Danielle.

"Hi, Maddie," Cameron said, tossing me one of his smiles that made the media swoon over anything he said on national television. I hated that smile. "I hope you don't mind the unexpected visit, but Sheriff Potts asked me to stop by."

With all that had been going on, I had momentarily forgotten that Cameron was working with the sheriff. Hadn't even considered it a possibility that he'd come knocking on my door. I wouldn't have answered otherwise.

"Now's not a good time, Cam. Come back tomorrow, will you?"

Cameron's smile didn't falter, and I remembered why I hated it so much. When we'd been married, if that smile ever emerged during an argument, I had known he thought I was being silly and he was just waiting for me to see reason. It was the smile he wore when he thought he was on a higher plane than the rest of us mere mortals.

"I know today's been really hard for you," Cameron said. "It will only be a couple of questions, I promise. Just some due diligence. Unless..." He paused and craned his neck, as if looking for something—or someone—just behind me in the house. "Unless Benjamin is uncomfortable with me being here. I mean, I can understand why he'd be intimidated—"

And then I did something I immediately regretted. I ordered him inside.

"Of course he's not intimidated by you," I said. "Why should he be?"

Cameron flashed his annoying smile as he walked past me. "I can think of a few things."

And we were back into our unhealthy habits, where Cameron said something he knew would get a reaction, and I couldn't help but oblige.

I'd been played, and he'd won this battle.

That didn't mean I couldn't win the war.

"You said you only have a couple of questions," I said, trying to take back control of the situation as I shut the door behind him. "So that's what you'll get. Two questions. Choose them wisely."

Cameron seemed taken aback by my bluntness—I hadn't ever pushed back when we'd been together—but he quickly masked it. He was ever the performer.

"Two questions," he agreed. "But first, I just want to tell

you how sorry I am for your loss, Maddie. Losing a father, even one you didn't know—that isn't easy. And in such a brutal manner, no less. If there's anything I can do for you or the kids—"

"I've been asking you to do things for me and the kids for years," I interrupted. "You were too busy. But now that my father has been murdered and you've somehow weaseled yourself onto the case, you want to be helpful. Forgive me, but I politely decline."

Cameron opened his mouth but then closed it again, apparently at a loss for words. He finally settled on, "I did try to help, when I could. You know how busy I am. I'm here now—that has to count for something."

We must have had a different definition of *help*. "I appreciated the child support, but now that the kids are moving out, I don't need anything from you, so no need to feel guilty about it."

He opened his mouth to speak again, but I held up a hand.

"They needed a dad. Someone who would visit on their birthdays, or at least call. You don't know what day it is half the time, let alone remember your empty promises of trips and time you said you'd spend with them. Your career and the attention you've garnered over the past few years has been more important to you than your children, and the least you can do is be honest about it."

Wow, that felt good. I didn't think I'd ever spoken to

Cameron like that—with Benji, I'd never needed to. And I finally felt free.

Cameron didn't try refuting my bold claims, though he looked like he wanted to. Instead, he pulled out his phone and flicked through a couple of screens.

He then held it up so I could see what was displayed.

It was a picture of my mom with Robyn. Not arguing. Laughing.

"This was taken yesterday," Cameron said. He then fell silent and let that sink in.

11

My mom had known that my dad was going to be at the wedding. Not only that, but she knew Robyn. And she liked Robyn.

The room spun, and I had to sit down. "That's not possible."

And yet it was—the evidence was right in front of me.

I looked up at Cameron. "How did you get that picture?" I couldn't even tell where it had been taken. Outside somewhere, from the looks of it.

"A source, who will remain anonymous, was taking pictures of the flowers around the hotel, and your mother and Robyn just happened to end up in the background of the photo. After today's events, my source thought it might be relevant."

I tried to ignore how smug Cameron looked as he

talked about his "anonymous source" and focus on the much bigger issue.

My mom had lied about having no contact with my dad and not knowing anything about Robyn. And then a terrifying thought hit me.

Had my mom invited Keith to the wedding? Why would she do that and then act shocked he was there, telling me and the kids what an awful and terrible human being he was?

"What do you know about Robyn, and more importantly, what is her relationship with your mother?" Cameron asked.

"You sure that's the question you want to ask? Remember, you only get two." I had to stall for time, my mind racing. Cameron knew far more than he should, especially considering the limited time he'd been here.

He nodded.

"You're going to be disappointed," I said. "Because when you showed me that picture, you should have realized I was just as surprised as you to see my mom and Robyn together. I don't know anything about their relationship or if they even have one. They could have randomly run into each other and struck up a conversation, all without having any idea who the other person was."

Cameron raised an eyebrow. "You really think that's plausible?"

"Just as plausible as my mom befriending her ex-husband's new wife."

Cameron's lips twitched up into a smile that brought back memories. It wasn't his superior smile or his snobbish grin. It was the endearing one—the one that had made me fall in love with him.

And I wasn't going to have any of it.

I folded my arms across my chest and nodded toward the door. "I've answered your two questions. If the sheriff has anything else she needs to ask me, you can send her my way."

Cameron's superior smile returned. "Oh, but you haven't finished answering the first question. I asked what you know about Robyn."

It was my turn to feel superior—because Cameron had made a mistake. "Your first question was actually two questions, even if you tried to sneak them in together. I answered one of them and then told you if I thought my answer was plausible. That was your second question." I opened the front door. "Tell the sheriff hi for me."

Cameron's eyebrows furrowed. There was obviously more that he wanted to ask me, but he didn't push further. Instead, he raised a shoulder in defeat and said, "I guess that's that. It's only your mom's freedom at stake, and if staying mad at me means more to you than clearing her name by answering a few questions, I suppose that's your prerogative."

In the past, that would have been all it took to make me

crumble, but I wasn't going to give in that easily. Those days were over.

"Like I said, I'm happy to talk to Sheriff Potts if she has further questions." And then I held Cameron's gaze until he looked away.

My chest constricted, my bold act of strength making me feel ill. I didn't want to stand in the way of the investigation, I really didn't. And if I thought it would be helpful, I would work with Cameron so that Keith's killer was brought to justice.

But I didn't trust Cameron. He was manipulative, and I didn't understand why he had chosen to stick around Amor, going so far as to offer his assistance to the sheriff, when he never had time for his own family. Now he seemed to have all the time in the world.

He grunted a goodbye but paused on the doorstep. "Did Flash show you the list we created of potential suspects?"

I knew it was another question, but I felt like answering this one. "Yes, he did. That was a good suggestion."

There. I had complimented him. That had been a very nice thing I'd just done. Maybe now Cameron could leave me alone.

When I didn't offer more information, Cameron rubbed his eyebrows. "Look, I'm only trying to help, and it was your sheriff who asked me to come. We'd appreciate it if you could at least tell us who your mom thought we should start with. Any little bit of information is helpful at this stage."

"That's very nice of you, considering you don't know a single person in this town outside our family."

Cameron understood the implication. That I didn't trust his motives—that I didn't understand why he was being nice. He frowned. "Sheriff Potts asked me to report back to her after speaking with you. It seems to me that you know who killed your dad, and you're protecting them. Is that what you want me to tell her?"

He watched me for a second longer, likely trying to gauge my reaction. When I didn't give him one, he spun around and left.

Cameron was trying to scare me into thinking that my mom was truly a suspect and that he had no problem implicating her for Keith's murder, and throwing me under the bus while he was at it.

Cameron didn't scare me—though I couldn't deny being worried for my mom. That picture was pretty damning evidence. I had a phone call to make, and it needed to be made before Cameron could do any more damage than he'd already done.

THE PHONE RANG three times before the sheriff answered.

"What were you thinking?" I asked Danielle, not giving her the chance to even say hi. "Why would you send my ex-husband to interrogate me? If you had come yourself, I would have gladly told you anything you wanted to know, but I don't trust him, and I'm not going to talk to him. If you—"

"Whoa, Maddie, slow down," Danielle said, interrupting my tirade. That made me more annoyed than I'd already been. "I never sent Cameron to your house to question you. When I said I'm working with him, I thought you understood that it's in a very limited capacity. I've asked him a few questions to get some insight into possible motivations for the killer, but Cameron doesn't even need to stay in town for that. He's a consultant—that's it."

My brain froze, and I wasn't sure how to respond to that. "You didn't ask him to come by my house?" I asked, numb.

"Did he say that I did?" Danielle asked, her voice rising in pitch.

I'd poked the bear, and she was awake and she was angry. Good. Now there were two of us who were mad at Cameron. I hated always being the only one.

"He absolutely did. Earlier today, he asked Flash to help him garner a list of people in town who would be old enough to have known Keith back when he was married to my mom. He also has a picture on his phone that he said was sent in by an anonymous source. Everything Cameron has been doing, he said he was doing with your blessing and that he was supposed to report back to you."

Danielle began swearing under her breath and then stopped, seemingly trying to regain her composure. "Can you come down to the station in twenty minutes? I have something I need to finish up first, but I need to know everything Cameron has told you or asked you, and everyone he's talked to. Who knows who else he's been getting information from, because he certainly hasn't been passing any of it on to me."

"I'll be there," I promised, and then I hung up.

My next phone call was to Benji to let him know where I was going and ask him to keep the kids away from Cameron.

When Benji answered the phone, I could hear a lot of background noise and what sounded like someone playing the trumpet.

"Benji, where are you?" I asked. Even if they were still at the diner eating ice cream, it shouldn't be nearly that noisy.

"At the park. Apparently, CJ has taken up the trumpet. He said your mom had hired him to play at our reception, but because that's not happening, he figured he'd give a free concert at the park. He's surprisingly good." He paused and pulled the phone away from his mouth while he talked to someone. When he came back, he said, "Cameron just walked up. He asked if the kids and I can give him a tour of the town. Before you say anything, I know you two have had your troubles, but with you and me getting married, I think it would be good if Cameron and I became friends, don't you?"

Oh, would this nightmare never end?

"Benji, listen to me very carefully. I know this is going to make me sound like a crazy, bitter ex-wife, but I don't want you spending time with Cameron. No tours. Don't answer any of his questions. And certainly, no investigating Keith's murder. I don't know what Cameron's up to, but—"

"Sorry, Maddie, but I can't hear you very well," Benji interrupted. "That trumpet... It's reaching notes that I don't think it's meant to."

"Don't let the kids spend time with Cameron," I half-shouted, hoping Benji could at least understand that. "He's up to something."

A pause as Benji pulled away from the phone again. "Sorry. I gotta go, Maddie. I know you're looking out for us, but Cameron just wants to spend time with the kids. We'll be back in a couple of hours. Enjoy your alone time."

And then he hung up.

I stared at my phone screen, not believing that my soon-to-be-husband had just hung up on me.

And then I released a scream of frustration.

Worst. Wedding day. Ever.

12

Last time I had visited Danielle at the sheriff's station, I'd felt sorry for her, being shoved away in the basement of Town Hall like that. It had looked more like an abandoned office space than a functional workplace.

This time when I entered, however, I was blown away by how bright and cheery it was. Rather than feeling like I was going down to the basement to be murdered, I could actually imagine myself choosing to spend more time down there.

The large space had been painted a calming shade of blue, large paintings covered the walls, and the flickering fluorescent lights had been replaced by recessed lighting. Danielle even had a proper desk now, as did her deputy.

Danielle was sitting at it now, scribbling furiously in a notebook.

"I love what you've done with the place," I said loudly,

in an attempt to announce my arrival. She hadn't yet noticed me.

She glanced at me and held up a finger, indicating I should give her a minute. I hadn't realized she was on a phone call.

"I see," she said into the phone while scribbling another note. "Harassment. Won't leave you alone. And you heard he was doing the same to Karla." A pause as she nodded. "Okay, CJ. I'll talk to him and figure out what's going on. I appreciate the heads up." Another pause. "Yup. You too. Better luck with your next concert."

Danielle hung up and leaned back in her chair. It was a fancy one—the kind that you would purchase if you wanted something ergonomic to improve your posture. I should have gotten one for my therapy office but instead had gone with the cheapest thing in the office supply catalog. I was regretting it now.

"Someone's harassing CJ?" I asked, finding another ergonomic chair at the next desk over and pulling it over. I collapsed into it, and it was as amazing as I'd thought it would be—like a down pillow for my lower back.

Danielle rubbed her eyes before spinning to face me. "Don't let Pierce catch you in his chair. Ever since we upgraded, that's become his baby."

"Pierce?" I had no idea who that was.

"Yeah, the deputy I hired six months ago. Can't keep a decent one around here for more than a year, but he's proving more reliable than any of the others. I hope he sticks it out."

"Can you blame them, with all the murders we've had around here the past few years?" I asked. "Amor used to be a safe place."

"I suppose I can't," Danielle said. "Anyway, Pierce is out taking statements from everyone who has called to complain about being harassed. Seems your ex-husband has been busy."

I groaned. The only time Cameron ever came to town was to pick up the kids for weekend visits, and the moment he's invited to stay longer, he manages to pull something like this.

"Who's been complaining?" I asked.

Danielle picked up her notebook and flipped back a few pages. "Several people at the hotel have complained about a man who fits Cameron's description hanging around and taking pictures. Victor—he lives on the next street over from you—said that a man of the same description trespassed and wouldn't leave his yard until Victor answered a few questions—questions that were nobody's business. When I asked what kind of questions, Victor refused to tell me. He did, however, go on a fifteen-minute rant about neighborhood kids who have been stealing lawn ornaments from his yard. Poor guy just wants to be left alone."

"And CJ?" I asked.

Danielle flipped a couple of pages. "He's the most

recent one. Said that during his trumpet concert, a guy was going around pestering people in the audience and distracting them from his performance. After he was finished, he asked around, wondering what was so important that the man couldn't wait until he was finished. Everyone told CJ the same thing—the man wanted to know about Keith. Specifically, what connections Keith had with folks in town."

"Of course Cameron did," I said, frowning. When Danielle raised a questioning eyebrow, I blew out a hard breath. "He convinced Flash to come up with a list of potential suspects and ask my mom to go through the names. Cameron wanted to know if any of them might still harbor a grudge against Keith. He then stopped by my house, under the guise that you had asked him to, and tried to get information out of me. Don't worry, I didn't tell him anything," I added quickly.

Danielle set the notebook down on her desk. "As much as I hate to admit it, that actually wasn't a bad starting point for an investigation."

I gave a humorless laugh. "Yeah, I know. I even told him so as an act of goodwill—to show him we're both on the same side. But the thing is, I don't know that we are. I have no idea why Cameron is still here or why he's taken it upon himself to find Keith's killer. He didn't even know the guy, and now he's going around town, asking questions he shouldn't be asking of people he doesn't know."

"And then there's the complaints about him taking

photographs around the hotel grounds," Danielle said. "For me, that's more than concerning."

The picture.

I knew I should mention the one that Cameron had shown me—the one proving my mom had lied about not knowing my dad was in town and that she didn't know his new wife, Robyn. But I needed to talk to my mom first. I was sure there was a perfectly innocent explanation—no need to bring the sheriff into it.

"What are you going to do about the harassment complaints?" I asked, hoping Danielle didn't notice the abrupt change of subject.

"I guess I could bring him in overnight—just long enough to make a point," Danielle said. "He needs to know that the town isn't going to put up with his shenanigans. We have plenty of nosy people in town who ask questions they shouldn't, but this town doesn't tolerate the same behavior from a stranger."

"No, we do not."

When I had first moved back to town, I'd been away for twenty years and had received the same treatment I would have as an outsider. I'd hated the small-town mentality back then, but over the past few years, it had grown on me. We took care of our own, and I didn't blame people for being suspicious of Cameron, especially when someone had just been murdered. At his ex-wife's wedding.

Danielle glanced at me. "I normally wouldn't feel the need to ask this, but is it going to be a problem if I choose to bring Cameron in? I don't want your kids breaking him out of jail in the middle of the night or something crazy like that."

Every ex-wife's dream. Giving permission for her ex-husband to spend the night in jail.

"It won't be a problem." This wasn't about revenge or payback. This was about discovering the truth. And if Cameron spending the night in jail helped deter him from messing with Danielle's investigation, then so be it. "And thank you for your help."

I stood to leave.

"Maddie, you're forgetting something," Danielle said, giving me an expectant look.

No, we had cleared up the situation about Cameron. He was going to spend the night in jail, and then, with any luck, he'd be heading home tomorrow. That was all I'd come for.

When it was apparent that I had no idea what she was talking about, she said, "The names of people your mom thought could have been involved in Keith's murder."

Oh, right. That.

I supposed if anyone had the right to know, it was Danielle.

I pulled the list from my purse and sat back down. "To be clear, my mom doesn't think any of them did it. She likes to think the best of people, even if she's happy to gossip about them."

"Of course," Danielle said, sitting up straighter and

picking up her pen, looking far too eager for the information I was about to give her.

I smoothed the piece of paper out in front of me. "It's interesting that CJ called you complaining about Cameron harassing him. I know my kids told you about the argument outside the church between Keith and CJ, and his was the first name my mom highlighted. It makes me wonder if Flash already gave these names to Cameron—why else would he be at CJ's impromptu trumpet concert?"

Danielle pursed her lips but wrote the name down. "It's possible. It doesn't help CJ's case that he had easy access to what could have been the murder weapon. I have my doubts it was him, but I can't count anyone out at this point. Next?"

I glanced at the list. "Karla Simmons. She apparently worked at the same sporting goods store that my dad managed and, when it was discovered that money was missing, he tried to pin the blame on her. They both ended up getting fired, but no criminal charges were filed because no one could prove who had done what."

"Karla Simmons," Danielle said as she wrote the name down. "I know who she is—she manages the hotel. Seems to have landed on her feet, so I don't know that she has motive, but maybe there's more to the story that we don't know." She looked at me. "Who else?"

I scanned the list for the next highlighted name. My gaze shot up and met Danielle's. "You said that a man named Victor complained about being harassed by Cameron. It wouldn't be Victor Bailey, would it?"

Danielle raised an eyebrow. "Yeah, it would. He's on the list?"

Now I was sure that Flash had shared the highlighted names with Cameron.

I swallowed hard and nodded. "Not only is he on the list, but my dad got into a fight with Victor's son and put him in a coma. A coma that his son never came out of."

And if I wasn't mistaken, it was the same guy that the kids and I had encountered earlier in the day. The one who just wanted to be left alone with his late wife's gnomes.

That couldn't be right. Maybe I'd gotten my names mixed up. Or there were multiple elderly men who lived on my street who complained about teenagers stealing their lawn ornaments.

"I could be wrong, though," I hurriedly added. "He's got to be in his seventies and he never leaves his house—"

Danielle snapped her notebook shut. "Actually, he's eighty years old, and he's a man who has lost everything— he literally has nothing and no one to lose. It looks like we have our prime suspect."

I wondered if it was too late for Benji and me to make the flight for our honeymoon—if Danielle sent that old man to prison, I didn't want to be anywhere near here when it happened.

Because it would be my fault.

13

I hurried after Danielle after making sure her deputy's chair was placed back exactly where I'd found it. "We don't have to do this now, do we? I mean, there's no evidence tying Victor to the murder, and I didn't see him at the wedding. How would he have gotten Keith to drink some kind of acid, anyway? It's not like Victor could have overpowered him."

Danielle looked at me as we waited for the elevator. "I'm not arresting him; I just want to ask him a few questions. The sooner we can get to the bottom of things, the better."

"Hasn't he been through enough for one day, though?" I asked. "Tomorrow would be just as good as today."

"Maddie, I understand you feel guilty that he's being suspected of such a terrible thing." Her expression was sympathetic, though her eyes were firm. "But don't think I didn't notice that you kept your mom's name off the suspect list. If it came down to it, would you rather your mom be the one that I'm looking closer at? The way I see it, she has nearly as much motive as Victor does."

If Danielle knew how much Keith had put my mom through, we'd probably be visiting my mom first.

"Once I'm done there," Danielle continued, "I will be informing your ex-husband of his new accommodations for the evening."

Meaning, the cell in the basement of Town Hall.

A terrifying thought occurred to me—one I hadn't even considered.

If she brought Cameron in, what would stop him from showing her the picture he'd taken? The one that raised a lot more questions about my mom's involvement with Keith and his new wife—questions I was unsure my mom could answer.

The elevator door opened, and we stepped in.

"Or we could leave Cameron out of it, for right now," I said. "I mean, his heart is in the right place."

Danielle studied me as the door closed and the elevator started moving. Her gaze didn't break until the door opened again. "You don't trust your ex-husband's motives, and a few minutes ago you had no problem with me locking him up for the evening, but now his heart is in the right place? You're not telling me something. What else happened when he visited you at your house? What did he say to you?"

I hesitated, not wanting to lie to Danielle. That brief hesitation was a mistake, and she picked up on it immediately.

"Maddie, I appreciate you stopping by and talking with me, but you are too close to this case." She stepped out of the elevator and then moved toward the front doors. "You're going to tell me whatever it is that you're trying to hide from me, and then you need to go home. Spend time with your family. You deserve it after everything you've been through today."

I really didn't want to tell Danielle about what Cameron had shown me. There had to be another way. But if I protected my mom and she really had done it, I knew the kind of trouble I could be in. Obstruction of justice and all that kind of stuff. And let's be honest, I wasn't made for prison.

Not only that, but the more I tried to protect my mom, the more lies I would have to tell, not to mention I'd have to somehow keep Cameron from speaking with the sheriff for the remainder of his time in town—which, at this rate, appeared to be indefinite.

The impossible situation weighed heavily on my chest, and I struggled to breathe. My vision swam.

Danielle rested a hand on my back, steering me outside and to a bench. "You're going to pass out if you don't sit and slow that heart of yours."

I squeezed my eyes shut and collapsed onto the bench.

"Focus on your breaths," she said, sitting next to me.

I followed her instruction, and as I did so, my breathing became more regular. When I opened my eyes, the world had stopped spinning.

Danielle folded her arms across her chest and leaned back. "Whatever you know," she said, "it's important. Otherwise, you wouldn't be having a panic attack. Something tells me it's something that incriminates your mother, and I'm assuming it's why you suddenly have a problem with me keeping Cameron overnight. You're afraid he's going to tell me everything you don't want me to know."

I'd said it before, but Danielle was not only good at her job, she'd also be fantastic at mine. Good thing she hadn't gone into psychology, or I'd be unemployed.

"My mom didn't do it," was all I could think of to say.

Danielle gave a small nod. "And I believe you. But without all the facts, it makes it that much more difficult for me to figure out who actually killed your dad." When I didn't respond right away, she released a sigh. "Look, even without whatever information you're withholding, I have enough to consider your mom a prime suspect, so I'd advise coming clean. It will be better for everyone in the long run."

Danielle was right. If I was going to help my mom, I needed to tell her everything.

"Cameron showed me a picture on his phone," I said.

"But it doesn't mean anything. A woman can have a conversation, can't she? It's not a crime."

"Who was she talking to?" Danielle asked.

"Robyn. My dad's new wife."

She nodded, like she wasn't surprised. "Arguing?"

I shook my head. "Laughing."

That got Danielle's attention. "Just after Keith was murdered, his former wife was laughing with his current wife."

"No," I hurriedly said. "The picture was taken yesterday. My dad was very much alive at the time."

Even with the added clarification, I realized what this looked like. When Cameron had shown me the picture, it hadn't even occurred to me that someone might think my mom and Robyn had planned my dad's murder together. And that they had been laughing about it.

Danielle started ticking off suspects on her fingers. "So, we have Karla, Victor, CJ, your mom, and Robyn who all could have killed your father."

That list wasn't nearly long enough for my liking. I felt like there was something I was forgetting to tell the sheriff. Something important that could help my mom. It was when Danielle began to stand that I remembered.

"Cameron didn't take the picture," I blurted out. "He said he received it from an anonymous source."

She glanced at me. "Was this at the same time he was telling you that he was asking you questions on my behalf?"

Oh, right. Cameron could have easily lied about the anonymous source and taken the picture himself.

"He'd only met my mom on a few occasions, and he had no idea who Robyn was," I said. "Why would he take pictures of them? It only makes sense that someone else did."

I'd made a good point, and Danielle didn't quite know how to respond. She studied me for a moment and then said, "I'll take that into consideration. In the meantime, I am going to do my job, and you are going to stay at home with Benji and your kids. You deserve a break on your wedding day. In fact, go on your honeymoon. I'm sure the pastor could perform a quick ceremony before you leave— make things official."

Leave town while there was a very good chance my mother would be wrongly arrested for murder. Not likely.

"I'll admit that there was a brief moment I considered it," I said. "But Danielle, we've known each other a long time. You know how much my family means to me, for better or for worse. I haven't always been there for my mom, and I've been trying to make amends. Do you really expect me to leave town at a time like this?"

Danielle sighed and shook her head. "No. But I'm serious about you staying out of it. I can admit that your insights have been very helpful in the past, but this case— it's personal for you. There's a lot at stake, and you can't be objective."

If I were her, I'd tell me the same thing. She was a good sheriff. The best this town had ever had.

That was what scared me.

What if I didn't like the outcome? It was hard to argue against someone who was smart and calm, and did their due diligence.

"Then I'll leave you to it," I said, and I stood to leave. "If you need a second opinion on anything, you know where I am—always happy to help."

Danielle didn't look convinced, her eyes narrowing in suspicion. "What are you up to?"

"Nothing," I said, attempting to sound like I really did plan on going home and settling down with a good book or watching a movie with my kids. "It's been a long day, that's all."

She didn't buy it, but I hadn't really expected her to.

"If you follow me, I swear—"

I held up a hand, stopping her. "I promise, I'm not going to follow you. You're right. This case is too personal, and I can't be trusted with it."

Now she really didn't believe me, but she had nothing to prove otherwise, so instead, she held up a threatening finger. Her lips moved, as if she wanted to continue her warnings, but nothing came out. Eventually, she gave up on trying to figure out what to say, and she turned in the direction of Victor's house.

"Do not follow me," she shouted as she walked away.

She didn't need to worry about that. I had been telling the truth—I wasn't going to follow her.

That didn't mean I was going home, though.

I had a different destination in mind.

And it had the potential to either be exactly what I needed or make everything worse.

I really hoped it wasn't going to be the latter.

14

I walked through the hotel's front doors and instantly wondered if this was a mistake. It wasn't just because Robyn was a suspect in my dad's murder and I knew Danielle would be furious if she knew I was here. The thing was, no one would approve of it. Not Danielle, not Benji—certainly not my mom. There was value in leaving things alone—leaving them in the past.

But I'd never been very good at that. And neither were my kids, which was why I shouldn't have been surprised to find them in the hotel's lobby.

"Mom," Lilly said, hurrying over and pulling me into a hug. "Don't be mad," she whispered.

Don't be mad. Right. Okay.

What I really needed to know was what I wasn't supposed to be mad about.

"We were getting ice cream, just like we'd told you we

were doing," she said, pulling me over to the couches where Benji and Flash were sitting. "But then Robyn walked into the diner and ordered some soup. I swear we didn't mean to eavesdrop, but she was talking really loudly. She was talking to someone on the phone, asking when her car would be finished."

"Which means she's been down to CJ's auto garage since arriving in town," I said.

Lilly gave a vigorous nod. "Yup. And from her side of the conversation, she's really wanting to head back home, but her car isn't finished yet. She was super angry and yelling at the poor guy. At first, she was going to dine in, but after she finished her call, she changed her mind and took her food to go. We were already done, so Flash and I decided to follow her. And she came here."

"That's not unusual, her coming back to where she is staying at the hotel," I said, though there was plenty about what they'd overheard that I was concerned about.

Benji raised a finger, looking guilty. "I know I shouldn't have let them drag me down here, but I swear they tricked me. And then we saw your mom entering the hotel not long after and—we're not saying that the two events are connected, but we were curious and thought we'd wait here until your mom came back down."

Okay, my mom being here was even more worrisome, and that was without Benji and the kids knowing about the photo.

Now I was torn. There had been wisdom in Danielle's advice to stay out of things. And I'd tried, I really had.

When I'd decided to come to the hotel, it hadn't been to investigate; I'd only wanted to visit Robyn. Find out the truth about my dad. I wanted to know if he'd really changed.

I guess what I had been after was closure.

My mom being here, though—that changed things.

"I promised Danielle I was going to stay out of things," I told them.

My kids laughed. Even Benji was smiling, like I had told a joke.

"I know this isn't how we expected today to go," Benji said, his smile dipping when he realized I hadn't been joking. "You know I want nothing more in the world than to marry you and whisk you away to Colorado for our honeymoon."

Flash crinkled his nose. "I still don't know why you chose Colorado. I mean, you could go anywhere, and you chose somewhere that is literally one state away. The only thing they have there is mountains. When I get married, I want to go somewhere exotic. Like Thailand."

Both Lilly and I looked at Flash in surprise. He had graduated high school without having gone on a single date, and it really had seemed like he couldn't care less about it.

"Stop saying stuff like that," Lilly told her brother. "It's freaking me out."

Flash seemed genuinely confused. "Say stuff like what, that I want to go to Thailand?"

"No, that you want to get married," Lilly said, like it had been obvious. "I can't imagine you taking care of yourself, let alone sharing a life with someone else. And kids? Forget it."

"Anyway," Benji said, trying to bring things back on track, "what I was trying to say was that today your mother and I were going to be married. Instead, she's been running around town in her pajamas trying to comfort your grandma while at the same time solve her estranged father's murder, and I can only imagine how difficult that must be for her. If she needs to take a step back and let Sheriff Potts handle things, then I support her in that."

Always my hero.

I walked up to him and planted a large kiss on his cheek. "I appreciate that, honey. I've honestly tried to stay out of things as best I can—I have no desire to be involved in this case. It's become nearly impossible, though, when everyone else seems to want me involved. People give me information I didn't ask for, and then I feel obligated to do something with that information."

"This isn't just about solving Grandpa's murder," Lilly said. "What about Grandma? She's in trouble, isn't she? I can't think of a better reason to stay involved."

Flash snorted. "The sheriff would never arrest Grandma."

Always the optimist. I gave him a sad smile. "Unfortunately, I do think your grandma is in trouble. And you're right, Lilly, she does need our help. But we need to go about it the right way, otherwise we could land ourselves in some real trouble."

Flash jumped up from the couch. "Well, we're not helping Grandma by sitting down here."

"Like I told you before, Flash," Benji said with a patient smile, "the hotel has a policy to not give out room numbers. They've been a lot stricter since a crazy fan attacked an actress who was staying here while waiting for her space tourism flight. After the attack, she threatened to sue the hotel, which would have bankrupted the entire place. Luckily, they were able to convince her otherwise, but the hotel doesn't make exceptions now. We'll need to wait for your grandma to finish with Robyn."

Flash didn't seem to think much of that idea, and he marched over to the check-in desk, where a young woman was looking bored and scrolling through her phone.

"Hey, Constance," Flash said, leaning against the desk. "Remember me from calculus? I was the only sophomore in the class."

She glanced up, her eyes lighting up in recognition. She straightened, a shy smile spreading across her face. "Sure, I remember you, Flash. I heard you graduated early and already got a job."

Flash beamed and leaned in closer. "You heard right. But hey, my grandma is staying at the hotel for my mom's wedding, and I don't remember what room she's in. Could you look that up for me?"

Constance's smile faltered, like she was conflicted about giving the cute boy what he was asking for or following the rules of the hotel. "I thought your grandma lived here in Amor," she said.

"One of my grandmas does. This is a different grandma. Most people have two sets of grandparents, you know." He said it playfully so she would know he wasn't trying to be rude.

Constance tucked a strand of hair behind her ear and smiled at him. I had to hand it to Flash, for someone who spent most of his time in his room on a computer, he had some unexpected skills with the ladies.

"I guess I could look it up for you. Just don't tell anyone," she said.

Flash glanced over his shoulder and gave us a thumbs up.

Way to be subtle.

Constance didn't notice, though, having turned to her computer.

"What's your grandma's name?" she asked.

"Robyn." Flash said it with confidence, but the girl looked up, not yet typing the name. "What?" he asked.

She smiled again, like she thought Flash was the greatest thing ever. It seemed that the same cluelessness that drove his sister bonkers was irresistible to girls not related to him.

"I need a last name, silly." Red spread across her cheeks, and her gaze immediately dropped.

I loved watching teenagers awkwardly flirt. I wished I had thought to record the entire exchange. If I ever had a bad day, it would cheer me right up.

But then Flash looked back at me, panicked. He didn't know Robyn's last name.

Robyn had mentioned when we'd first met that she had kept her maiden name. I thought back, trying to remember what it had been.

Carter.

But how could I pantomime the name Carter?

I spotted one of the hotel's luggage carts and pointed to it. Flash glanced toward it, then turned back to the desk.

"Trolley."

Constance raised an eyebrow.

"Robyn Trolley," he repeated.

She still didn't type, looking perplexed. When Flash glanced back at me, I didn't know what else to do to help him, but then her features relaxed, and she laughed.

"You're funny," she said. "And as it turns out, we only have one woman named Robyn staying with us right now. Robyn Carter. Is that her?"

Red moved up Flash's neck, and I knew he was embarrassed, but he was good at hiding it. "Sorry, yes, that's my grandma Carter. We have an inside joke, because in Great Britian, they call carts trolleys, but I've been calling her

Grandma Trolley so long, sometimes I forget it's not her real name."

Constance laughed again as she scribbled something down on a piece of paper and handed it to Flash. "Your grandma is in room 403."

Flash thanked her, and then Benji, Lilly, and I joined him at the elevators.

"Constance gave me her phone number," he whispered. He wore a smile that would put the Cheshire Cat to shame.

Lilly turned back. "I really should warn her."

I grabbed her arm and pulled her onto the elevator with us. When the doors closed, I let go, then turned to Flash. "I'm not surprised that she likes you—you're a smart, good-looking guy."

Flash's blush deepened. "Mom, stop. I probably won't even call her. I'm leaving in a month, remember?"

Yes, unfortunately, I did.

Lilly glanced at Flash, wearing a smirk. "It's probably for the best. She thinks you're a lot fancier than you really are. Since when do you use terms like trolley?"

"That wasn't my fault." His voice was tinged with annoyance. "The only frame of reference I have is from listening to my rich friends that I meet through online hacking competitions. Do you know the last time I stayed in a hotel?" He shook his head. "It wasn't even a hotel—it was that rundown motel at the hot air balloon festival, and it was not the kind of place that has luggage carts or trolleys, or whatever you call them."

If I didn't know better, I'd think Flash was embarrassed by it. But that kind of thing had never bothered him before.

The elevator dinged when we reached the fourth floor, and the doors opened. We didn't make it into the hallway, however, before we heard a loud bang. And then a scream.

Benji and I whipped toward each other, our expressions panicked, then we ran out of the elevator.

In opposite directions.

"I swear it came from this direction," I called to him. The kids had taken sides, Flash coming with me and Lilly going with Benji.

Benji shook his head, then pushed the door nearest him with his toe. It swung open easily. "Unfortunately not," he said.

Flash and I ran back to where Benji and Lilly stood. Room 403. Lying on the floor was Robyn, blood soaking her shirt.

"She could still be alive," I said, kneeling next to Robyn and placing my fingers on her wrist. "Come on," I whispered. It took a minute, but I found a pulse. "Got it."

When I turned back to tell Benji to call an ambulance, he already had his phone out. His hands shook so hard, he was having trouble dialing.

"Here, let me," Lilly said softly, taking the phone from

him. She called dispatch and gave them all the necessary details.

I turned to Flash. "I'm going to try to stop the bleeding. I need you to help Benji sit down. He looks like he's going to pass out."

Flash did as I asked, and once Benji was safely sitting on the floor, he turned to me. "Does this mean what I think it does?"

I raised an eyebrow. "What do you think this means?"

Flash threw a nervous glance behind him before turning back. "Grandma shot Robyn."

15

Grandma shot Robyn.

Those words echoed for several long seconds before I could answer Flash.

"We don't know that," I said. "And when Sheriff Potts asks about what happened here, we will tell her exactly what we saw. Which was nothing. We heard the shot, but we didn't see who held the gun."

"And when she asks why we were coming to see Robyn in the first place?" Benji asked.

That one was easy enough.

"Her husband—my father—was murdered today, and the poor woman doesn't know a soul in town. We came by to check on her and make sure she's all right."

Benji and the kids murmured agreement that Sheriff Potts wouldn't be able to argue with that.

It didn't take long for the paramedics to show up.

Thankfully, because of the construction of the spaceport and all those celebrities who stayed in our town before their space tourism flights, a proper medical facility had been built. A few years earlier, Robyn would have died before the ambulance ever made it to town.

Soon after the paramedics arrived, Sheriff Potts stepped out of the elevator. When she saw it was us who had made the emergency call, she stopped, her eyebrows furrowing.

"You cannot be serious. I told you to go home, Maddie. You promised. And yet, I didn't even manage to finish speaking with Victor before I was called with news about another murder.

"Attempted murder," I corrected. "Robyn is still alive, for now."

I should have kept my mouth shut. Danielle looked like she wanted to pummel me over the head.

"What are you doing here?" she asked through gritted teeth.

I pulled in a quick breath before giving the excuse we'd practiced. "My father—her husband—was murdered today," I said, like it should have been obvious. "We stopped by to check on her and make sure she was doing okay."

"Uh-huh." Danielle glanced at my kids, who were eagerly nodding, affirming the truth of my statement. She turned her attention back to me. "Did Robyn know you were coming?"

I shook my head. "Unfortunately not. She has my number, but I don't have hers. In fact, we had to get her room number from the front desk."

Danielle didn't look like she was buying a word of my carefully crafted story. "The hotel has a policy against that."

"We're very persuasive."

That seemed to be the first thing I'd said that the sheriff believed, but she pretended to be shocked by the admission.

"You don't say," she said.

I chose to ignore her sarcasm.

Danielle stepped aside as the paramedics moved past us, pushing Robyn on a stretcher. She now had an oxygen mask, and the paramedics were applying pressure to her wound as they walked quickly toward the service elevator.

Danielle turned her back on me as she spoke into her radio, and her deputy arrived just a short moment later.

"Take pictures and gather samples," she told him. "I want everything by the book."

My kids craned their necks, trying to see around the doorframe and into the hotel room.

"You two, back up," Danielle barked at them.

Their gazes snapped to her, their eyes wide, and they dutifully stepped back. I'd never heard Danielle yell before, and certainly not at my children.

"They weren't touching anything," I said, my voice soft.

Even though I preferred they not see blood-soaked carpet, I doubted it fazed them. They'd seen worse.

Danielle spun back toward me. "I don't care. Everywhere you go, people die. In this case, two people in the same day—on your wedding day. So, excuse me when I say that if it were up to me, you'd leave town. Right now. And not come back until this was resolved."

I stared. Danielle had had her frustrations with me in the past, but she'd never been mean. We were friends. I'd thought.

"I know it's been a rough day," Benji said, stepping forward. "But that's uncalled for. You know that Maddie had nothing to do with—"

Benji was interrupted when Danielle's deputy stepped toward the sheriff, a small evidence bag in hand, and he whispered something that I couldn't hear.

Her gaze snapped to me as she gave a curt nod. "Finish up here," she told him. "I'll meet you back at the station."

The deputy's gaze lingered on me for a brief moment before he re-entered the hotel room. Whatever was going on, it had to do with me.

"What did he find?" I asked.

Danielle motioned for me to follow her. There was nothing more for us to see here, and I needed an answer to my question, so I did as she asked, even if I wasn't happy about it.

"But—" Flash and Lilly simultaneously protested.

"You heard the sheriff," I interrupted. "Let's go."

When we'd all entered the elevator and the doors had closed, I repeated the question. "What did your deputy find?"

Danielle refused to answer, remaining silent for the entire ride down. She wouldn't even look at me. When we had all exited the elevator, but I didn't move to leave the building, she glanced over her shoulder. "If I find you anywhere near my suspects, including your mother, I'm arresting you."

And then she left.

"What was that all about?" Flash asked. "She was grumpier than usual."

I supposed two murders in one day could do that, but I had a feeling there was more to it than that.

Rather than answer Flash, I pulled out my phone and dialed my mom's number. Benji and the kids had seen her enter the hotel, but no one had seen her leave. I needed to make sure she was okay.

The phone rang for what felt like forever before it eventually went to voicemail.

"She always answers her phone," I murmured. "Even when she's not supposed to." I glanced at my watch. Five-thirty.

I turned to the kids. "We're going to see Grandma and invite her to visit the hospital with us. It would be a nice gesture for all of us to be there when Robyn wakes up."

"Are you sure that's wise?" Benji whispered to me. "Your mom and Robyn are the sheriff's top suspects, and you heard her. As crazy as it is, if you go near them, she'll arrest you."

"Robyn was just shot," I said. "I doubt she's still considered a suspect. And if there's ever a time for family, it's now. In whatever form that comes."

Benji studied me, his brows knit in concern. "For someone who wanted nothing to do with your dad or Robyn a few hours ago, that's a quick turnaround."

My voice dropped in volume. "I think it will be the safest place for my mom right now, and it's the last place Danielle will look for her." I paused and glanced at my kids, who were watching us, obviously trying to catch what I was saying. "The way Danielle wouldn't look at me or answer my questions—the way she yelled at us, wanting us to leave town. That wasn't frustration or annoyance."

"You think the sheriff's deputy found something that can link your mom to the shooting," Benji said.

I nodded. "And she believes we'd be willing to tamper with evidence. Anything to save my mom." I hesitated. "I think Danielle is on her way to arrest my mom right now. And we need to get there first."

16

Benji's work truck was not meant for three people, let alone four. He was sitting in the driver's seat, and Lilly and I were scrunched on the bench seat. Flash was now trying to slide his way inside.

"Just sit in the bed of the truck," Lilly complained.

"No way," Flash said. "There are all sorts of sharp tools back there. One turn taken too quickly, and I become a shish kabob. That is not the way I want to go."

The boy had a point. Benji always threw his tools and other supplies he needed for his handyman jobs back there.

"He's right," I said. "It's too dangerous."

Lilly harrumphed as she tried to position herself sideways so there was more room. "And you think we're going to fit Grandma in here if we can't even get Flash in?"

"Maybe I should run home and get my car," I told Benji.

Benji gave me a long look. "If you really think Danielle is on her way over to your mom's house to arrest her, we won't get there in time."

"Good point. We can take my mom's car to the hospital. I'm sure she won't mind."

In the end, Flash ended up sitting on my lap, folded over so he was resting his arms on the dashboard. As soon as we were mostly settled, Benji turned the key in the ignition, and we sped away from the hotel.

"I don't understand why it couldn't be Lilly who sat on your lap," Flash complained as he tried to protect his head from banging against the top of the cab. "She's smaller than I am."

Yes, that would have made more sense, but by the time we'd thought of it, it had been too late.

"Another speed bump is coming up," Benji warned, then pulled onto a side road so he could drive faster.

It wasn't fast enough.

As we rounded the corner of my mom's street, the sheriff's car was pulling away. And in the back was my mom. She saw us through the window and waved frantically as she mouthed one word—HELP.

Benji slowed the truck down, eliciting protests from the kids.

"What are you doing?" Flash yelped. "Grandma needs us."

Benji glanced at them, his gaze sympathetic. "We can't help her if the sheriff sees us—especially after we were explicitly warned not to come anywhere near her suspects."

"But that's not a suspect," Lilly said. "That's Grandma."

"Yes, but unfortunately, she's both right now." I grimaced and looked at Benji. "I think I need to do something that I'll regret later."

Benji nodded. "Do it."

I gave him a curious look. "You don't know what it is yet."

"You need to call Cameron and ask for his help," Benji said, matter-of-fact, like calling up my ex-husband on my wedding day to ask for help in solving two murders was the most natural thing in the world. Well, one and a half murders. The second one was still up in the air.

I nodded. "It's just that he was out harassing everyone on our suspect list, which means he may have information we need. I doubt Danielle is going to bother keeping him overnight at the station now that she has my mom in custody."

"You don't need to convince me," Benji said. He reached over Lilly to hold my hand. "Right now, he's our best chance at figuring out what's going on here. Let's go talk to him."

Lilly looked uncomfortable with the act of intimacy she was stuck in the middle of, and she pushed our hands apart. "Isn't Dad staying at the hotel as well? He's probably there right now."

That was right. Which meant another member of my family could be placed at the scene of the shooting. Or at least in the general vicinity.

That wasn't good.

I immediately changed my mind about involving Cameron any more than he already was. "You know, it's getting dark. Maybe tomorrow would be better."

Unfortunately, Flash had grown impatient from sitting on my lap, and the next thing I knew, he was on the phone with Cameron.

"Hi, Dad. Grandma was just arrested and the sheriff told us to leave town, but we're going to prove her innocence instead. Want to help?"

Looked like we were doing this the Swallows way—recklessly and without a plan.

Why not? It wasn't like this could get any worse.

THIS WAS SO MUCH WORSE than I'd thought it would be.

We were all back at my house—if the sheriff had the inclination to check up on us, she'd see both my car and Benji's truck parked in front. She didn't need to know that we'd picked up Cameron along the way.

Flash and I had chosen to walk from the hotel. It had been best for everyone involved. It had given Flash the chance to stretch, and it had prevented a third murder that day. If I'd been scrunched up in that truck with Cameron and he'd mentioned one more time how we had done the right thing to come to him, I would have snapped.

Now we were all seated around the dining room table, empty pizza boxes thrown off to the side. I shifted uncomfortably on my seat, wishing we could all move somewhere else, but then that might prolong this conversation, and that was something I could do without.

"I think there are two different murderers," Cameron said. "Serial killers don't usually use multiple methods."

"But women tend to use both poison and guns, right?" Flash said. "Couldn't it be the same woman?"

Cameron lifted a shoulder. "Could be, though men use guns far more than women do. The poison makes sense for Keith's murder because of the public nature of it. It's a lot easier to get away with it, but how did they get him to drink the poison in the first place? It would have to be someone he trusted in order for them to get close enough to get the substance into his water bottle. That would imply Robyn. Which begs the question—if she didn't kill Keith, why would the real murderer mess things up by then attempting to kill her? It doesn't make sense. She was the perfect scapegoat."

The dinner conversation we were having now was very much like the ones when Cameron and I had been married, and it was triggering all sorts of memories I'd thought I'd buried in the recesses of my mind.

"You're right, it doesn't make sense," I said. "That's

probably why the sheriff is so frustrated." I was trying to stay calm, but not knowing what evidence the sheriff had against my mom was making that really difficult right now.

I retrieved a piece of paper from a drawer in the kitchen. "No one in town would have met Robyn before she arrived, so I think we need to focus on what motive someone would have had to kill Keith and circle back to her later. We also need to take into account what opportunity our suspects might have had."

Cameron glanced at me. "Sure, that's something to consider." And then he resumed his thoughts on which gender was more likely to use that particular type of poison, and how he still thought it could be two different murderers. Possibly a man and a woman working together.

"I'll be back in a minute," I said abruptly, shoving my chair back from the table. I stood so quickly that the chair teetered precariously on its two back legs, and I had to lunge to keep it from toppling over.

Everyone looked at me and then kept talking.

Everyone except Benji.

He followed me out of the room and onto the front porch. "Everything okay?"

I shook my head, close to tears. "I don't know why I thought this was a good idea. Cameron craves attention and will do anything to get it. The work he does—it's not about helping anyone. He does it because studying the psychology of serial killers is sexy. It sells books and gets him TV gigs. Never mind that he lost his family because of it."

Benji took my hand in his. "I get it. This is the last place you want to be, with the last person in the world you want to be spending time with. We were supposed to be in Colorado by now, and instead your long-lost father crashed your wedding right before he was murdered, your stepmom that you didn't even know existed has been shot, your mom is in jail, and we're sitting around the kitchen table with your ex-husband, trying to figure out how to fix everything. If I didn't know better, I'd think the plot was written for daytime television, but it was so unbelievable— even for a soap opera—that they couldn't air it."

That earned a smile from me. It was small, but it was something.

"So, what do we do?" I asked, leaning into him. "As if things weren't bad enough, the sheriff has warned that if any of us so much as go near her suspects or the crime scenes, we'll be arrested."

Benji wrapped his arm around me. "Yes, that's a conundrum. The good news is that the only thing we need to worry about right now is proving that your mom didn't do it—we can let the sheriff take care of the rest."

"What's the bad news?" I asked, twisting so I could see him better.

Benji grimaced. "The bad news is that all of the evidence points to her doing it."

17

Before Benji and I re-entered the kitchen, I made a promise to myself. Whatever my feelings toward Cameron, my mom was more important. If he could help cast doubt on my mother being a murderer, I could be nice and work with him for however long it took for her to regain her freedom.

I pulled in a deep breath and followed Benji back to the table.

"Mom, we made a chart," Lilly said, holding up a large piece of poster board left over from a failed experiment that Flash had entered into the school science fair. Flash had wanted to test how different materials reacted when placed inside a microwave. He'd tried everything from hard candies to Styrofoam. We went through a lot of cleaning supplies that week.

Despite Flash's precision in recording data for each item, and the high grade he'd received for the project, I considered the experiment a failure.

Because my son had almost killed us.

Flash had been smart enough to not put aluminum or any other kind of metal inside the microwave, but as the final experiment, he'd decided to microwave chile peppers, and then planned on frying them up after to use in enchiladas. It sounded good. The only problem was that the microwave had caused the peppers to release an ungodly amount of capsaicin into the air, sending us running outside as our eyes and throats burned.

Even after opening all the doors and windows in the house, it was two hours before we could return inside.

And now we were using the back side of that experiment's poster board to organize murder suspects.

It was fitting.

At the top of the chart, Lilly had written MOTIVE and OPPORTUNITY. Along the left side, she'd listed four names.

VICTOR

ROBYN

CJ

GRANDMA

"Do we have to include Grandma?" I asked.

Lilly nodded. "We need to be able to show this chart to the sheriff to prove Grandma didn't do it, which means we need a side-by-side comparison."

I looked to Benji for help, but he merely shrugged. "She has a point. Danielle won't release your mom without a good reason."

"Fine," I grumbled, then turned back to the chart. "Victor has the strongest motive. Keith put Victor's son in a coma, and he died three weeks later."

Anger welled in my chest. The thought of someone doing that to my kids—it was unfathomable. And to think that my own father had done that to someone else—it made me physically sick. When I had gone to the hotel to visit Robyn earlier, I had wanted closure. But every time I thought of the people my father had hurt, I didn't think that was possible. Maybe he had changed, but he could never make up for what he had done. Not to my mother. Not to Victor. No one.

Someone else had figured that out a lot quicker than I had, and they'd taken matters into their own hands.

Under MOTIVE and next to VICTOR, Lilly wrote, KILLED SON. "That's so sad. I can't believe Grandpa did that." She moved to the next section. "What opportunity did Victor have to give Grandpa the poison?" Her hand hovered over the space, waiting for us to tell her what to write.

"Victor didn't come to our wedding," I said. "And I doubt he knew that Keith was even in town—the man never leaves his house. I don't think he could have done it."

Lilly frowned, then wrote, NONE.

Cameron leaned back in his chair. "That's not good if

the person with the strongest motive had no opportunity to commit the crime."

I glanced his way, and I jutted out my chin in defiance. "I'm glad he didn't do it—he's a lonely old man who wants to live the rest of his life in peace. Is that so bad?"

Benji rested a hand on my shoulder. "Cameron has a point," he murmured in my ear. "I know this is hard for you, but we need to work together."

Cameron studied me for a moment. "I'm not trying to step on any toes, Maddie. I understand that this is your town and you know it far better than I do. But every time we cross someone off that list, it's another step toward your mom being convicted herself."

Benji was right—Cameron had made some good points. As much as I didn't want someone like Victor or CJ to be a murderer, I'd prefer that to my mom being locked up for the rest of her life.

And really, if Victor had done it, no one would blame him. I doubted a jury would convict him once they heard his story.

"You went over and talked to Victor. Did you get the sense that he might know more than he's saying?" I asked Cameron, hoping to convey that I didn't intend to fight him every step of the way, even if that meant fighting against my own natural inclinations.

Cameron shook his head. "Unfortunately, no. He was outside and yelling at me before I'd made it halfway to the door. Before leaving, though, I managed to talk over him and ask one question: if he'd ever thought of killing Keith Lawson."

My kids leaned forward, their expressions eager.

"What did he say?" Flash asked impatiently.

Cameron looked between them in a dramatic fashion. "Victor went silent, and then said, 'Every day for the past forty years.' And then he slammed the door on me."

Flash and Lilly both gasped, the reaction I was sure Cameron had been looking for, and I held in an eyeroll.

"It strengthens the case for motive," Benji said, "but there's still no opportunity."

Flash pulled out his laptop and began typing furiously. "Hang on," he said. "I remember noticing something when I was looking into Victor earlier." He paused, then pointed at the screen. "There. Victor has frequent doctor visits. Because...you know...he's old. And guess when his last one was?"

"I bet I know," Lilly said. "This morning. During the wedding."

"Before the wedding, but yes," Flash said. "Dr. Harris closed his office during the actual ceremony. Most businesses in town were closed so they could attend. Victor was his only appointment of the day."

I raised a shoulder. "So what? Victor had a doctor's appointment, and then he returned home. That doesn't help us—he wasn't at the wedding."

Flash held up a finger, telling me to hold on. "He wasn't at the wedding, but Dr. Harris's office is right around the corner from the church. Victor would have had to pass the church when he drove home." He then gave me a triumphant grin. "Opportunity."

18

I t was a stretch, at best, but I had to hand it to Flash, he was good at helping raise reasonable doubt. That was all my mom needed.

Reasonable doubt.

Proof was better, but I'd take what I could get.

"Okay," I said. "Write it down."

Lilly wrote next to Victor's name, DR. APPOINTMENT NEAR CHURCH.

"What are our thoughts on Robyn?" Cameron asked.

We all paused. It felt wrong to consider her a suspect now that she'd nearly died herself. We still didn't know if she was going to make it.

"Maybe we should skip this one," Lilly said, her pen poised.

Cameron gave a quick shake of his head. "No, we need

to consider all angles. What if she killed her husband, then felt such remorse that she tried to kill herself?"

"It's too dramatic," I said. "Besides, people who do that, they don't shoot themselves in the chest, do they?"

Benji spoke up, and to my surprise, it was to defend Cameron's theory rather than mine. "I don't think we should discount it as a possibility. If she was shot point blank, there will be documentation of it."

Flash was already on it, typing away on his computer, and I chose to not look at his screen. I didn't want to know which database he had to hack into. "No data yet," he said. "Should be soon."

I stared at Benji for a moment, not understanding why he would suddenly be siding with Cameron.

Benji leaned in close, his voice low. "You don't need to look at me like I killed your pet rabbit. There are no sides here, and I think we need to consider all possibilities, no matter how unlikely."

"So, you do admit it's unlikely," I pressed.

He gave me a patient smile. "It doesn't matter. Everything is a theory right now. We've seen stranger things, haven't we?"

I supposed we had, and Sheriff Potts had always thought I was out of my mind when I'd presented my theories to her before, even when they had proved true.

"All right," I said, my voice at normal volume. "I'll admit that it's just as good a theory as anything else we've got right now." I nodded to Lilly. "Write it down."

Lilly turned to the poster board to write, but hesitated.

"What?" I asked.

She turned back to me. "It's just that...well, there wasn't a gun."

I straightened. "What do you mean? There had to be. We all heard the shot."

Lilly gave a vigorous nod. "Yes, I know. Robyn was shot. But in the hotel room, there was no gun. When Flash and I peeked inside, the deputy hadn't gathered evidence yet—we would have seen it."

Benji's gaze whipped to me. "She couldn't have done it."

"Robyn is no longer a suspect," I said. "Cross her name off."

Lilly didn't hesitate this time as she drew a line across Robyn's name.

Cameron folded his arms across his chest, his gaze on the table. "I'm sorry, Maddie."

I raised an eyebrow. "For what?"

His gaze lifted. "If we don't think that Robyn could have shot herself, and your mom was seen in the hotel moments before the shot fired—"

I stepped back and raised a finger. "Don't you dare."

Benji looked between us in confusion. "Don't he dare what?"

My gaze stayed on Cameron, my heart racing in anger. "He's treating this like the case is closed. That's what he wanted—he's probably going to write a book on it. Use my mom for profit. He's done that to other families—why not mine? Doesn't matter if she's guilty or not, as long as he comes out ahead."

Cameron had the audacity to look bewildered at the prospect. "Maddie, I would never do that—"

"I've read your books. The case studies," I said, interrupting him. "I've also heard about the lawsuits. Even though you changed the names, it didn't take long for people to start being identified by their friends. Neighbors. Some have received threats. All have been ostracized. All because they had the misfortune to be related to someone who did terrible things. Guilty by association. I won't allow you to do that to my mom. Or your kids."

Cameron held up a hand. "I've only ever written the truth. And I truly thought their identities would be protected."

Benji touched my sleeve. "Maddie, maybe we shouldn't do this here." He nodded to where Lilly and Flash were watching us, their expressions shell-shocked.

So much for my rule to never speak ill of their dad in front of them.

Guilt replaced my anger, and I collapsed into the nearest chair. "I'm sorry. That was unfair. I just—this is my mom we're talking about. She's not a murderer. And you're right, they are going to think it was her. My mom is the only person who had opportunity to both kill Keith and attempt to kill Robyn. I thought reasonable doubt would be enough. It won't be. Without evidence that someone else did it, my mom is going to spend the rest of her life in prison. Even after death, my father is still ruining her life."

Benji walked up behind me and placed his hands on my shoulders, giving them a reassuring squeeze. We were beyond words at this point—there was nothing left to say—but he wanted me to know he was there for me, no matter what happened.

"Contrary to what you believe," Cameron said after a long moment of silence, his hands fidgety as he averted my gaze, "I'm not here to write a book, and I'm not here to pretend I know everything. I am also not here to convict your mother. I only wanted to point out that we have an uphill climb ahead of us, so you need to prepare yourself. Things might not turn out in her favor."

I slammed my hands down on the table, the anger returning. "Don't you think I know that? I know how bad it looks, considering our only other prime suspect was shot in her hotel room an hour ago. That leaves us with an elderly man who rarely leaves his home and would have had to have the foresight to bring poison with him to his doctor's appointment, and a mechanic who Keith owed money. So, unless you can find some pretty damning motivation for CJ to kill both Keith and Robyn—because killing someone isn't the way to get your money back—I know where that leaves us. With my mom in prison."

Everyone stared at me in shock.

"You never lose your temper," Flash whispered. "Even when you're mad, you never yell."

"Well, maybe I should yell a little more often," I said, even as I pulled in a long breath, trying to calm myself. "Because my life has been one disaster after another, and I have had to keep my emotions in check through it all. The only bright spots have been you two." I looked at Flash and Lilly. My gaze then landed on Benji. "And you."

Cameron frowned. "I'll try not to take offense."

I glanced at him. "You can take some offense."

"Maddie," Benji warned. He could tell that I was in one of my moods. I didn't get like this often, but when I was tired and overwhelmed and completely dysregulated, who knew what I would say? I'd regret most of it tomorrow morning.

I held up my hands. "You're right. This is why Danielle didn't want me near her suspects. I'm unpredictable, and that's the last person you want near a murder investigation." I spun toward Cameron. "But you've had contact with the suspects. All of them. You've been talking to so many people that Danielle has received complaints about you."

Cameron studied me. "You say that like it's a good thing."

"Yeah, because you have information the rest of us don't."

He raised a shoulder. "People in your town don't trust strangers, let alone the ex-husband of their therapist. Victor wouldn't talk to me, I didn't get much of a chance to talk to CJ because he was playing that blasted trumpet at his impromptu concert, and no one in the crowd was any help. They all said the same thing—that they were a peace-loving town who wouldn't wish harm on another human being, even someone who had done them wrong."

Flash snorted. "That has not been our experience since moving to this town."

He wasn't wrong.

"They didn't mention any names at all?" I asked.

Cameron began shaking his head but then paused. "A few did mention feeling sorry for Victor, the past being brought back the way it was. They found it cruel. And they did express sympathy for your mom—apparently Keith was quite the womanizer back in the day, and they weren't at all surprised that he'd return forty years later with a new wife. They found it completely inappropriate."

I nodded slowly, my gaze resting on the poster board. I groaned, then stood from the table. How idiotic of me. "We forgot about Karla."

"Who?" Cameron asked.

"Karla," Benji repeated. "She works at the hotel and sells green chile at the farmer's market on the weekends." He glanced at me. "What connection does she have with Keith?"

I turned away from the board. "She worked with my dad at the sporting goods store when the company auditor discovered that quite a bit of money had gone missing over the previous months. My dad said it had been Karla who was stealing, but the sheriff was never able to find definitive proof against either of them, even though they were the only ones who had the opportunity, so the company covered their bases by firing both of them."

Benji's eyes lit up in realization. "And she would have had access to both Keith and Robyn at the hotel."

"She doesn't just work at the hotel. She runs the entire place," I said.

Flash solemnly nodded. "Motivation and opportunity. I think we found our killer."

19

"You can't just storm into the hotel and accuse Karla of murdering two people," Benji said, running after me.

I unlocked my car and slid into the driver's seat. "Yes, I can. Danielle told me to stay away from her suspects, and Karla isn't one of them. At least, she's not a serious one."

Benji held my door so I couldn't close it on him. "Then tell Danielle about your suspicions. Let her take care of it. She doesn't want your mom to be guilty any more than you do."

I glanced at Benji's hand. "Let go, honey."

His expression remained resolute, even as Flash and Lilly clambered into the back seat.

I turned to face them. "No."

They responded by leaning back and crossing their arms over their chests, their lips pressed in firm lines.

"You're not too old for me to ground you," I threatened.

They laughed, then resumed their positions of rebellion.

"Fine," I said, releasing a long sigh so they knew I wasn't happy about it. I glanced up at Benji, who was still blocking my door from closing. "You coming?"

He hesitated as Cameron opened the passenger door and slid into the car.

My gaze whipped to him, then back to Benji, who looked completely calm about the situation. In fact, it seemed like he and Cameron had planned it.

"Are you serious?" I said. "Cameron should not be the one coming with me."

Benji nodded slowly. "I know. But he's staying at the hotel, so if the sheriff is giving you grief about being there, you can use him as an excuse."

"And let me guess, it was Cameron's idea," I said, turning to Cameron.

He gave me an embarrassed smile. "What can I say? I'm full of great ideas."

"You're full of something," I muttered as I stuck the key into the ignition.

Benji leaned down and kissed me, I was sure more for Cameron's benefit than anything, and then shut my door.

I watched his retreating figure in the rearview mirror as I pulled away from the house, because this whole situation right now—Cameron sitting next to me, the kids in the back seat—it almost felt like when the kids had been younger and we were going away for the weekend.

And it felt wrong.

"You're going to let me do the talking when we get there," I said.

Cameron lifted his hands. "Of course."

I glanced his way. "Why are you being so agreeable all of a sudden?"

"I'm always agreeable. You've just never noticed."

I snorted.

Cameron turned to me, looking serious. "I know I've made mistakes, Maddie, but haven't you punished me enough? I've lost track of how many times I've apologized and—"

I held up a hand. "Stop. We're not doing this here." I glanced into the rearview mirror at Flash and Lilly in the back seat. They were pretending they were absorbed in their phones, but I knew they were hanging on to every word.

"I'll follow your lead," Cameron said, his voice turning quiet. The curtain had been lifted, and he was no longer the cocky celebrity psychologist. In this moment, he was the man I had first met—the man I had married.

Whatever shadow had been cast, once in a while I was reminded of the good days we'd had. And the kids deserved to have those days as well.

"Thank you," I said. "And for what it's worth, I do value

your insights." I paused. "I appreciate you staying. My mom needs all the help she can get."

Stunned silence filled the car.

"You don't have to act like I've never been nice before," I grumbled.

Cameron cleared his throat. "You're welcome. I'm happy to help."

I pulled up in front of the hotel and parked the car.

"Here goes nothing," I said, though realizing it was a very big something.

And I was not looking forward to it.

"What is our plan?" Cameron asked as we entered through the front doors.

I gave him a blank stare.

"I'm following your lead, remember?" he prompted.

Right. That implied I had a plan, even though I'd run out the door the moment I'd realized Karla was most likely our murderer, without thinking what I was going to do about it.

"The less you know about the plan, the more natural it will seem," I said, as if this made any sense, and then I marched up to the front desk.

The same young woman that Flash had flirted with earlier in the day, Constance, was working the desk. "Hi," I said. "We need to speak to your manager about the room we are staying in."

Apparently, this was the plan.

Constance's eyes widened slightly. "Is there a problem? Your satisfaction is important to us and—"

"I understand," I said. "I know you're doing your best. But we really need to speak to your manager."

The poor girl looked like she might be near tears, likely terrified that we were about to get someone in trouble, and I immediately felt bad about it. But then Constance straightened and looked me in the eyes, her voice firm and confident. "I'm sorry, but Ms. Simmons leaves at six o'clock every evening. I can help you, though."

I glanced at the clock. It was nearly seven-thirty already.

An older woman, probably in her late sixties, appeared through a door behind the front desk, wearing an almost genuine smile. It was her eyes that gave her away. They were dark brown, and a storm brewed behind them.

"It's all right, Constance. I can take care of it." The woman turned her attention to me. "I'm Karla Simmons, the hotel's manager. You'll have to excuse Constance for covering for me. I stayed late to catch up on paperwork and asked her to pretend I wasn't here."

Karla looked different than I had expected. Every hair was in place, her dress perfectly ironed and her makeup expertly applied. Almost like the strict nannies from *Mary Poppins*—the ones that gave you nightmares as a child.

"Hello, Ms. Simmons. I'm—"

"Please, call me Karla," she interrupted. "And I know

who you are. You're Laurie Lawson's daughter." Karla extended a hand, then glanced at Flash and Lilly. "And of course your two children. I've heard a great deal about the three of you—it's big news when anyone leaves Amor. And even bigger news when they come back." She ignored Cameron completely.

I shook her hand. "Yes, as I've learned from experience." Like when the town council had made me prove my loyalty to Amor when I'd returned with Flash and Lilly after a twenty-year absence. I nodded to Cameron. "This is Cameron. He's a guest at your hotel."

Karla was finally forced to acknowledge him and gave him a tight smile. "I hope the accommodations meet your expectations. I know it's not fancy, but it's comfortable."

Cameron hesitated. "The room is fine, thank you."

"Fine," Karla repeated, like the word tasted bitter. "It sounds like your stay with us could be improved. Perhaps you'd enjoy breakfast in our on-site restaurant tomorrow, on us, of course."

"I appreciate that," Cameron said. "But my concerns go beyond my room and your restaurant." He paused. "Is there somewhere more private we can talk? It's a delicate matter."

Karla's eyebrows rose as she studied him, but then she motioned for us to follow her into an empty conference room. She shut the door behind us and gestured to one of the empty tables. "Please, have a seat."

We each sat down, but Karla remained standing, her

arms crossing her chest. "I know about your family," she said. Her stance had turned aggressive, and her voice pierced the silence of the large conference room. She glanced at me. "You, your mom, your kids—you all follow the same pattern. Rebellion. Deceit. Why are you really here?"

I glanced at Cameron. For someone I'd never met before, Karla sure seemed to have a lot of opinions on our family. I should have started looking into this woman the moment I'd heard about her connection with Keith.

"This is because I dated Keith, isn't it?" she said when I didn't answer right away.

I blinked. "Wait—you—"

"Dated your dad," Karla finished for me. "And we would have been engaged if your mother hadn't come along." She said it matter-of-factly, no emotion in the statement.

"You dated my father, before he married my mother," I said, my brain trying to catch up. "You must be very angry—him choosing someone else over you."

Karla leaned against the edge of the next table over, studying us. "Was I angry? Yeah, for a while. But the way I see it, I dodged a bullet, didn't I?"

My brain was reeling with this new information, and right now, Karla was the one controlling the narrative. I needed to take that control back.

"You tell yourself that you dodged a bullet—it makes things easier. But I don't think you really see it that way," I said, leaning forward and meeting her gaze. "I think you loved Keith enough to kill him for what he did to you. It was my mother you hated—it was her fault he left you. But then he left us too."

Karla remained silent, neither confirming nor denying my words, so I continued.

"You couldn't believe it when, a couple of days ago, you saw him check in to your hotel with his new wife. A blast from the past—and not the good kind. All that pent-up anger that you thought you'd managed to rid yourself of bubbled to the surface, and you hatched a plan. You would kill Keith and then pin the blame on my mom. The perfect revenge. Except, after his death, my mom wasn't arrested." I leaned back. "You needed evidence that was so damning, Sheriff Potts would have no choice but to put her behind bars. That's why you shot Robyn. Might as well get rid of the second wife while you're at it, right?"

"Maddie," Cameron said, his voice soft as he touched my leg. "I don't think that—"

Karla interrupted him. "No, it's all right. I got this one." When she turned to me, her expression had softened and she was smiling like she knew something I didn't. More than that—she looked like she was on the verge of laughing.

"That's why you dragged your family down here?" she asked. "Because you thought I was so angry at Keith that I felt the need to destroy the lives of anyone connected to him?"

I stared. "Well, yeah."

Lilly leaned over and whispered in my ear, "Karla is wearing a ring."

I had no idea what she was talking about until my gaze landed on Karla's index finger. There, indeed, was a diamond ring. A very large one, in fact, especially for someone who had never left Amor.

"You're married," I said. "Who's the lucky guy?"

"Engaged, actually," Karla said. She held up her hand, her gaze resting on the ring. "Why would I throw away my life on an ex-boyfriend from forty years ago when I have one now that is a thousand times better?"

That was a good question. "Because Keith did nothing but hurt you. Not only did he leave you and marry my mom, he got you fired from your job. Doesn't that kind of person deserve to be punished?"

My kids' gazes both snapped to me in shock at my bluntness, but the time for dancing around the truth was over. Karla seemed like a shoot-from-the-hip kind of woman, and I needed to meet her where she was.

Karla's lips parted in surprise, but then her eyes crinkled in amusement. "Is that what you heard? That he got me fired?" Her expression fell just as fast. "It was the other way around. I'm the one who got him into trouble."

Cameron and I shared confused looks.

"He wasn't the one stealing money from the sporting goods store?" I asked.

"No." Karla's gaze landed somewhere on the other

side of the conference room, as if she were reliving a painful memory. "We had both worked at that store for years. Whether we were dating or we'd broken up, we were always at that stupid store, together. Neither of us had anywhere else to go. But I wanted more from my life than selling fishing poles and tennis rackets, so—this was after he'd married your mom—I started skimming money just before I'd take the deposit to the bank at the end of the day. I needed a nest egg to escape, and I wasn't ever going to do it on the wages they were paying me."

"But my grandpa found out," Lilly said, her voice quiet.

Karla glanced at her and gave a little nod. "He covered for me, because he knew he wasn't going anywhere—he had a family now—but he could help me get out of Amor." Her breath shuddered. "He was fired because of me. He went out drinking because of me. And he got into that stupid fight that left Danny Bailey in a coma because of me."

She shook her head, her gaze rising and meeting mine. "I was serious when I told you I'd dodged a bullet. After Keith was fired, he changed. Don't get me wrong, he'd never been a family man, so I don't know why he thought he'd try it on for size. He'd always been a drinker, always been a gambler. But it was after I had gotten him fired that he really went downhill. In a way, I feel responsible for everything he did from that point forward. And I felt sorry for your mom, having to put up with all the crap he pulled." She pushed off from the table. "I didn't kill Keith, and I didn't shoot Robyn."

Well, that was a bust.

"One last question, if you don't mind," Cameron said, his voice soft but firm. It was the kind of voice that made you trust him, even if you weren't sure you should. "Who do you think most likely killed Keith?"

Karla didn't hesitate when she said, "Victor Bailey, and no one would blame him for it." She walked to the doorway to the conference room and held an arm out in a gesture that said we were meant to follow her out. "We're done here."

"We're close, I can feel it," Cameron whispered to me as we left the room, an excited gleam in his eye.

"Sheriff Potts said to stay away from Victor," I said, throwing an anxious glance at the front desk, as if someone were listening and was going to tell on us.

Flash snorted. "Since when do you listen to the sheriff?"

"Since your grandma was arrested. If we unintentionally do something that jeopardizes the investigation, it could be very bad for her—and us."

That put everyone in a somber mood as we exited onto the street.

It was a warm evening. I was sure Colorado looked beautiful right now, the rugged mountains contrasting sharply with the starlit sky.

A man shouted from across the street, breaking

through my reverie. I turned to see CJ, illuminated by the streetlamps, waving in our direction, and then striding toward us.

"We can't talk to him," I said, panicked. Danielle was my friend, but if she thought we were purposely going behind her back—

Cameron placed a hand on my shoulder. "We can't avoid everyone in town." And then he gave a bright smile as he turned to our mechanic. "CJ, just the man we were hoping we'd run into."

20

CJ was a man who was likable enough but preferred cars to people. He always said that his first love was cars and his second love was his tabby cat, Lucky Charm. The rest of us... We were further down the list.

"This is serendipitous, running into each other," CJ said, crossing the street to join us. He looked at me. "I've been trying to get ahold of you."

I pulled my phone out and glanced at the screen. Sure enough, four missed calls from CJ and another seven from Trish.

"Sorry, I forgot to take my phone off silent after the wedding," I said, holding up the phone to prove it.

I felt bad that I'd missed his calls, but I felt worse about missing Trish's. She'd always been the person to make sure I was okay after a day like today, and she was probably beside herself with worry. Ever since she'd moved out of the house a couple of weeks earlier, things had felt off, and I missed her.

"It's lucky for us as well," Cameron told him. "I've been looking forward to meeting you."

CJ didn't even glance his way. I wondered if Cameron knew that CJ had complained to the sheriff about him.

"What can I do for you?" I asked CJ.

"Keith's car," he said. "I need it gone from my shop."

I stilled. "Now's not the best time. I'm sure you heard what happened to his wife, Robyn, at the hotel."

"Yes, terrible tragedy," CJ said, truly looking sorry about the situation. "The thing is, I finished their repairs, and I need to make room for other vehicles."

I rubbed my eyebrows, the stress of everything weighing heavily on my shoulders. "CJ, Robyn is in the hospital, and I haven't been given any updates on her condition. Can't you hold onto it for a little longer? Just until we can figure everything out."

CJ hesitated. "I really don't have the space, Maddie. As Keith's next of kin—"

"I know," I snapped. "But the dad that I met for the first time today is dead. His wife has been shot, my own mother has been arrested, and I haven't been allowed to see her yet. Things are a little busy right now."

My kids' gazes dropped, and CJ looked shocked at my outburst.

"I'm sorry," I said, my voice dropping to just above a whisper. "Things have been stressful. If you need me to pick their car up, I will, but can it wait until morning? It's been a long day, and I'm exhausted."

CJ hesitated but then gave a small nod. "Of course. The morning is fine. Thank you."

"Glad we got that settled," Cameron said. "While we have you here, CJ, you knew Keith back in the day, didn't you?" He said it like it was an afterthought, then flashed his signature smile. The one that made people do anything he asked—the one that melted them into putty. "I'll bet you have all sorts of stories."

I turned a glare on Cameron. Right now wasn't the time to try to get information out of CJ—I didn't want to scare him off.

CJ was quiet for a moment, then turned to Cameron. "I hear you've been asking a lot of people about Keith. Stuff that's none of your business."

Cameron looked surprised at CJ's hostile tone—it was rare that someone wasn't taken in by his charm. "The thing is, Maddie's family is my business. Keith was her father and my kids' grandfather. Helping them find closure isn't nearly enough to make up for my past mistakes—my past absences. But it's something."

CJ studied Cameron a moment, as if trying to determine if Cameron was being genuine or not. I had to admit that even I wasn't certain about Cameron's authenticity—I generally erred on the side of not. But CJ must have seen something different, because he nodded, then turned back to me.

"Maddie, if you're looking for closure, I don't think you want to hear the stories I have about your father. It sounds like he was trying to make a change for the better, and that should be the memory we preserve."

His reluctance to speak ill of the dead was understandable, but I was certain my father's death had everything to do with his past, and that meant digging in the mud, no matter how painful.

"I need to know," I said, holding CJ's gaze, my voice quiet. "Was he as bad as everyone says?"

CJ ran a hand through his hair, like he was uncomfortable with the question. "Your dad..." He hesitated. "Yes. He was as bad as you've heard. When Keith put the Bailey boy in the coma, we had had enough. Never mind all the debts he still owed everyone. We just wanted him gone."

"You mean, you weren't the only one he owed money to?"

CJ gave a quick shake of his head. "Oh, no. Back then, it was difficult to find someone who Keith didn't owe money. Whether it was the owner of the bar for damages, his boss at the sporting goods store for all the money he'd stolen, or people he'd simply borrowed money from, everyone had a story."

"And what's your story?" I asked.

He rubbed his chin, his gaze flitting to Cameron.

"We can go to the diner to talk if you would feel more comfortable with that," Cameron said, giving him a kind smile.

Flash grinned. "Finally. I've been starving for the past two hours but was afraid to say anything."

CJ's lips twitched up at the edges. A chime sounded, and he pulled out his phone, glancing at the screen. "I'm afraid you'll need to wait a little longer," he said to Flash. He looked at me apologetically. "The diner closed twenty minutes ago, and I need to be getting back to the shop."

I knew it was getting late, but I hadn't realized how late.

"Of course," I said, though internally I was panicking. With the sheriff's warning to stay away from the investigation, this was likely my last chance to ask CJ what had happened between him and my dad. His answer could be the difference between my mom's freedom and her going to prison for the rest of her life.

"I do need to warn you that Sheriff Potts knows about your and Keith's argument outside the church this morning," I hurriedly said as CJ turned to leave. "If you could tell us what happened between you two, we might be able to help."

CJ turned back to me, his expression hard and his voice gruff. "That conversation was private."

"In a very public place," I said.

CJ's eyes narrowed. "You're saying that Sheriff Potts wants to pin Keith's murder on me, after all I've done for this town? Well, I don't have to prove anything to anybody, and I resent the implication." He then turned and walked away, his strides angry. "I want Keith's car gone by eight o'clock tomorrow morning," he called over his shoulder.

My heart dropped as I watched his retreating figure. "Sorry, that was my fault."

Cameron rested a hand on my shoulder. I was sure it was meant to be comforting, but it had the opposite effect on me, and I shrugged it off.

"You handled it better than I would have," he said, acting like my rejection to his touch hadn't affected him. I could see the hurt in his eyes, but I ignored it. I had more pressing matters on my mind.

We weren't going to get anything else out of CJ, but there were other suspects out there. Including my mom. Regardless of the sheriff's warnings, I was tired of this waiting game—feeling so helpless, while my mom's fate was in someone else's hands.

"Well, what's done is done," I said. "What we need is a good night's sleep. First thing in the morning, we'll pick up Keith's car, and then we are driving over to the sheriff's station to ask my mom what exactly happened when she went to the hotel."

"But you said—" Lilly started.

I shook my head. "You can forget everything I said. We have a grandma to rescue."

21

The next morning didn't come quickly enough. I tossed and turned the entire night, anxious to get a start on the day. My mom was going to be furious we'd allowed her to spend the night at the sheriff's station. Without any substantial evidence that someone else had shot Robyn, though, I didn't know what else I could have done.

I glanced at my phone. Seven o'clock. I slipped out of bed and downstairs so I wouldn't wake anyone, then grabbed my purse and stepped outside. After all the chaos of the previous day, today I felt like being alone.

The morning was crisp and quiet—a perfect start to the day. I hadn't walked farther than my driveway, however, when I heard the front door open, then slam shut.

I pretended I hadn't noticed and continued walking, turning left on the sidewalk toward CJ's garage.

"Beautiful morning for a walk," Lilly said, catching up and matching my pace.

"Perfect," Flash agreed, appearing on my other side.

As much as I loved my kids, I had expected to have this time to myself—alone with my thoughts. I pulled in a long breath. I wouldn't have many more days like this before they moved away, and I knew I was going to miss it.

I smiled, grateful that they even wanted to still spend time with me.

"You two are up early," I said.

Lilly threw me a side glance. "We knew you would try to sneak off without us, so we've both been awake for the past hour, waiting for you to leave."

"You could have told me, I'd have made you breakfast."

Flash snorted. "Yeah, and then you'd try to talk us out of coming. You think we wanted to miss out on seeing Grandma in jail?"

I should have known there was no way they'd allow that to happen.

"It's not that I didn't want you two to come," I said. "It's just that Danielle... Well, you know how sensitive she is when it comes to you two and her investigations."

"I don't see why," Flash said. "We've helped her so many times, we should be on the payroll."

"True," I said, my words slow. How to put this... "I think it's mostly due to you tampering with evidence and illegally hacking into databases. You know—things that could get her fired if they were ever to come to light."

Flash waved a hand through the air, like I was being overly dramatic. "Those are the things she loves most about us."

I didn't know what to say to that, and Lilly laughed. "Don't try to make it make sense, Mom."

That was wise advice.

We turned a corner, and the rundown building that housed CJ's auto garage came into view. It was then that I heard someone calling from behind us. I didn't think it was Benji—he'd already told me he had taken several jobs around town so he wouldn't be so far behind when we were finally able to go on our honeymoon.

I glanced over my shoulder to see Cameron stepping out of his rental car. I didn't even bother to hold in my groan.

"He just wants to help," Lilly said.

I looked between her and Flash—neither of them looked surprised that their father had joined us.

"You coordinated this?"

Flash nodded, and Lilly looked guilty.

"Don't be mad," she said. "We only have a couple more days with him, and it's been fun having him along for the investigation."

I couldn't fault them for wanting to spend more time with their father, but I would have preferred they chose one of the many activities in Amor that didn't involve murder. Things like hiking or miniature golf.

Although, knowing our luck, they'd find a body on the eighteenth hole.

"And how do you think your grandma will react when she sees him?" I asked. She'd never liked Cameron, and for him to see her behind bars—she was going to be furious.

"It will be fine," Lilly promised, then turned as Cameron joined us.

"Did I miss anything good?" he asked.

I stayed silent, so Flash answered in my stead. "Mom tried sneaking out, but we were too smart for her. She didn't make it past the front yard."

Cameron laughed. "I raised you two right." He glanced at me, an eyebrow raised. "You didn't want them to visit your mom?"

"No, and I don't want you there either," I said. "Do you understand how serious this is? The kids and I—we've been in sticky situations in the past. But this feels different. If Sheriff Potts doesn't find evidence that someone else killed my dad and shot Robyn, there is an actual possibility that my mom is going to be locked up for the rest of her life." I paused. "I'm scared."

I stopped in front of CJ's auto shop, moisture pooling in my eyes. The garage door was open, but there was no movement. "If things go wrong, I want Flash and Lilly as far from it as possible."

"Oh, Mom," Lilly said, and then she and Flash crashed into me from both sides, hugging me as tight as they were able. A rare moment of solidarity between the two, and it broke the dam that had been holding back my tears.

"We're sorry for causing you more stress," Flash said, his words muffled by my hair. "I mean, in all honesty, we would have still followed you. But that doesn't mean we're not sorry about it."

I laughed and pulled back. "I know."

"Would you rather we go somewhere else with Dad for the day?" Lilly asked, though I could tell she really wanted to come with me.

I wiped at my eyes. "No, it's all right. You're already here."

Lilly and Flash grinned like they'd hit the jackpot.

"You know—" Cameron said, but then CJ poked his head out from the open garage.

"Morning. I appreciate you coming over so early, but are you four planning on coming inside? I just need you to pay for the repairs, and then you can be on your way."

"Sorry, CJ. We're coming," I said. "But when you say pay for the repairs..."

CJ had told us we needed to pick up my dad's car, but he'd never said anything about payment.

Cameron rested a hand on my arm. "Don't worry. I got it."

I wanted to protest. Cameron thought we were poor and couldn't afford it, so he was gallantly swooping in with his bank account to save the day.

But truth be told, things had been tight lately, especially with paying for a wedding and reception that hadn't happened, and I could really use the help. So I grunted a "thank you" and let Cameron do the right thing for once.

While he paid, I took the keys from CJ and was directed to an old red Toyota that had seen better days.

"Can I drive it home?" Flash asked, his eyes eager.

I hesitated.

Flash immediately saw it and frowned. "I'm a good driver."

I honestly had no idea if he was or not, hence the hesitation. We only had the one car, and we walked almost everywhere we went, so even though Flash had a license, he hadn't had much use for it.

"Better for him to practice now than have to figure it out when he moves to California," Lilly pointed out. Her reasoning was valid, but Lilly had the same problem—neither of them had much experience on the road.

"You're right," I said. "From this point forward, until you move, I will be treating the two of you as my chauffeurs. Whenever we want to go somewhere, even if it's only to Grandma's, you'll be taking turns driving me."

Lilly had been the more resistant to driving of the two, and she rounded on me in horror. "Oh no, Mom, I really don't think that's necessary. I'll be living within walking distance of my job."

"Is that how you're going to capture all your lovely, award-winning photos—shooting everything within one square mile of your apartment?" I asked.

She shifted uncomfortably. When she couldn't think of a good answer to that, she frowned and folded her arms over her chest. "Fine. But I get to choose the music when I drive."

Flash groaned. "She's been on an Enya kick lately. She's going to put us all to sleep—herself included." He then grabbed the keys from my hand and jumped into the front seat of the red Toyota. "If she gets to pick the music when she drives, so do I. Which means we're listening to Rammstein on the way home."

Great, my only choice for music over the next few weeks was going to be lullaby music or German heavy metal. It could be worse, I supposed. It could be country.

"Hey, Mom," Flash said, bending over to the passenger side and picking something up from the car's floor. "There's a notebook in here. Looks like a bank ledger." He straightened in the seat and handed it to me.

I flipped through the pages.

This was no bank ledger, though each page was filled with numbers.

If I wasn't mistaken, these were debts. It included names. And there were a lot of them.

22

Cameron walked over, having finished paying for the repairs. "CJ made it sound like it would cost a lot more than it did. Apparently, Keith and Robyn had complained of weird noises—tapping and rattling, that kind of stuff. It started a couple days ago, not long after they'd dropped off their luggage at the hotel. They thought they'd check out the ghost town on the outskirts of Amor, but when the noises started, they drove here instead. Turns out it was just a couple of loose bolts, as well as low oil. CJ only charged me for the oil change and did the bolts for free, as well as double checked to make sure there weren't any other issues."

"I'm glad it wasn't anything serious," I said, my attention still on the pages. I didn't recognize any of these names. "With low oil, it could have turned into something a lot worse."

"CJ said that it seemed it might have been intentional."

My gaze shot up. "What?"

"Couldn't find any leaks, and the oil that was in there was clean, which means they had an oil change fairly recently."

"Someone purposely drained the oil," I said, my words slow. My mind spun—we were missing something.

Keith and Robyn had driven into town two days ago, the day before my wedding. They had rested up a bit at the hotel and decided to go out sightseeing, but had car problems and stopped at CJ's.

My mind returned to the hotel.

I felt like it was key to everything. Robyn had been attacked there. The car problems had started after checking in there.

And there was Karla.

After speaking with her the previous evening, I'd crossed her off as a suspect, but maybe I'd written her off too soon.

"What do you have there?" Cameron asked, nodding to the notebook in my hand.

I shrugged, like it was no big deal. The idea of Cameron looking through it bothered me, though I hadn't made sense of it yet myself. It was the old knee-jerk reaction again, even when it was to my detriment.

It's for your mom, I told myself.

"Flash found it on the floor of the car," I said, handing it to him. "At first it looked like it might be everyone Keith owed money to, but there are too many names, and the dollar amounts are far too high. No one would loan him money in those amounts—and why would he need them to? There are multiple loans every day." I pointed to the first page that Cameron was looking at. "These ones are all crossed off, but as you get closer to today's date, they aren't."

Cameron's lips formed a tight line. "These aren't debts that Keith owed. These are debts that are owed to him."

I stilled. "What are you saying?"

He hesitated. "I've studied a wide variety of killers," he started.

I gave a sigh of exasperation. "Yes, I know, we were married and we worked together. I'm very aware."

"Please let me finish."

I pantomimed zipping my lips shut and gestured for him to continue.

"At first glance, it seems Keith might have been a bookie—taking bets for people on various sporting events. But these loans are happening every day in varying amounts—some are tiny, and some are astronomical."

Flash swung his legs out of the car and sat on the edge of the seat. "So, if he wasn't a bookie, what was he?"

Cameron seemed nervous for the first time as his gaze moved from Flash to me. "I hope I'm wrong, but he could have been a loan shark. Didn't want to have an electronic trail, so he recorded it all here in this little notebook."

"Loan shark," Lilly said, her voice soft. "Like those

people who break people's knees if they don't pay them back?"

Cameron nodded. "I haven't studied loan sharks in depth, but their psychology seems to be simple—greed and violence. They trick someone into taking a loan from them—the unfortunate guy doesn't know they are dealing with a loan shark—and then, because of illegally high interest rates, it is nearly impossible for him to ever get out of debt. These sharks—they aren't afraid to kill, or threaten to kill, to get what they want."

I thought back to how my dad had put the Bailey boy in a coma. Had he owed my dad money?

"We need to see if Robyn is awake and able to talk," I said abruptly. "Find out what she knows. Because if he's a loan shark, then she lied about him changing his ways. There is no way she wouldn't have known."

"Is it possible that he had other people doing the dirty work for him?" Flash asked. "They could have been out terrorizing his customers while Grandpa was at home having a chicken dinner with his wife."

A double life. That thought was terrifying.

Lilly frowned. "Going to the hospital and demanding to speak to someone we saw wheeled out of the hotel just yesterday with a gunshot wound? I don't know... It feels..."

"Wrong," I finished for her. "You're right, I don't know what I was thinking."

Cameron frowned. "Your mom might go to jail for the

rest of her life for something she didn't do. If talking with Robyn can prove her innocence, then that's what you need to do."

"But it won't prove her innocence," I said. "If Robyn tells us that Keith was indeed a loan shark, it will prove that my dad was a scumbag. But it won't prove my mom's innocence. Who's to say that he wasn't already a loan shark all those years ago when they were married?"

We were interrupted by CJ poking his head around the corner of the shop. "Sorry, I thought you'd left. Is there anything else I can do for you? Because I have a car on its way, and it needs to be in that exact spot when it gets here."

"Just leaving now," I said, giving him an apologetic wave. "Lilly, why don't you drive your dad to the house in his rental car, and I'll have Flash drive Grandpa's car. That way we'll only need to take one car to the sheriff's station when we visit your grandma."

"As in, I have to be the one behind the steering wheel?" Lilly asked, her face paling.

"You'll be fine," Cameron said, slinging an arm around her shoulders. "With me sitting next to you, nothing can go wrong."

I sincerely hoped that was true.

"Hey, CJ," I said, turning back to him. He was watching us, like he was making sure we were actually leaving. "Do you know if my dad was involved in anything illegal? I know he owed you money and that kind of thing, but did he ever loan out money?"

CJ laughed, until he realized I was serious. "Maddie, that man never had more than ten dollars to his name."

None of this made sense.

"Thanks, CJ," I said with a little wave, and slid into the passenger seat.

Flash sat in the driver's seat, looking a bit too comfortable as he fastened his seatbelt and turned up the bass on the stereo.

Here went nothing.

"Let go of the door," Flash said, annoyed. "I'm driving the speed limit, and there are no cars on the road for me to crash into. You're fine."

That was true, and we'd only hit two curbs so far. What I needed was a distraction for the three-minute ride home. And I got it in the form of a phone call.

From the sheriff.

She probably had her deputy out spying on us and he'd seen that we had visited CJ's.

"We're not going near any of your suspects," I said before she could even say hi. "We only went to CJ's shop because my dad's car was there, and he asked us to pick it up."

A long pause.

"Okay, duly noted," she said. "That sounds more like a guilty conscience, but I'll let it slide for now because your mom is asking for you."

"You said I can't go anywhere near her."

Never mind that we had planned on seeing her anyway, with or without the sheriff's permission.

"I didn't mean that you couldn't visit your mom in jail," Danielle said, her voice tinged with annoyance. "That would just be cruel, and honestly, a neglected Laurie Lawson is not a happy Laurie Lawson. I need you to visit her as soon as possible."

Meaning it was fine, as long as we were supervised. "Okay. I need to just swing by the house—"

"When I said you need to visit her, I meant you need to come now," Danielle said. "She's been lecturing me for the past twenty minutes on cruel and unusual punishment and has been detailing her rights as a citizen. At this point, I think she's just quoting every legal drama she's ever watched."

That sounded about right.

I didn't like that Danielle felt she could order me around, especially because she had made it very clear that she didn't want me or my family anywhere near her and the investigation.

In the past, it wouldn't have bothered me, because I would have done what I pleased and figured it was easier to ask forgiveness than permission. But I couldn't afford to be on her bad side right now—not when the stakes were so high.

And to think I'd thought the sheriff and I were friends.

"Fine. We'll be right there," I said, then hung up.

"Who was that?" Flash asked, glancing toward me.

I tightened my hold on the door handle. "Eyes on the road."

Flash gave an impressive eye roll, but his gaze returned to the road. "So, who was it?"

"Sheriff Potts. She says we need to come to the station straight away—apparently, she's having some trouble with your grandma. I need to call your dad and let him know of the change of plans."

Cameron answered on the second ring. Lilly had gotten them home safely, thank goodness, but he'd had to leave her there and was no longer at the house. He wouldn't give me a straight answer as to why, just that he had some stuff he needed to do.

When I called Lilly to tell her that Flash and I wouldn't be home for a while, she did not take the news well.

"I'm always left out of things," she protested.

"It wasn't intentional," I said, and then promised her pizza for dinner.

"It's Flash who loves pizza. I like tacos."

Right. Even with only two kids, I struggled getting things right.

"I'll get both pizza and tacos," I promised her, and then hung up as Flash pulled up to Town Hall.

Flash attempted parking along the curb but acciden-tally drove onto the sidewalk, barely missing a fire hydrant. Thankfully there were no other cars on the road this early in the morning.

I told him not to bother re-parking and jumped out of the car, knowing Flash would be close behind me. We opted for the stairs in lieu of the elevator and half-sprinted into the sheriff's office.

"And for another thing," my mom was shouting when we stepped into the room, "that lazy, no-good ex-husband of mine had so many extramarital affairs, how do you know the murderer isn't one of his mistresses back for revenge?"

I grimaced and looked at Flash. He did not need to hear any of that.

Rather than being traumatized, like I currently was, he took her suggestion seriously, nodding as he grabbed a piece of paper from the nearest desk, as well as a pen.

Danielle walked in from the next room. "Glad to see you could make it. That's my desk you're stealing a pen from, by the way."

Flash ignored her and hurried across the long room to where my mom was being held. The holding cell was in the far corner, and, even though I couldn't see her from where I was standing, the acoustics in this place were amazing. It was probably why Danielle had taken a break in the next room. With the door closed.

"Hallelujah, I'm being rescued," my mom said. "Took you guys long enough."

"Sorry, Mom," I said, hurrying to join Flash. "I had been told that I wasn't allowed."

"I never said such a thing," Danielle called across the room.

I glanced over my shoulder. "Agree to disagree."

Flash pulled out the pen he'd borrowed from the sheriff's desk. "About these mistresses. You didn't mention any of them before now, which I see as a dereliction of duty, but it's no use dwelling on that now. Do you have names for me?"

He placed the piece of paper against the wall, pen poised, ready to write them down.

"Does this mean you don't know who Keith and Robyn's killer is yet?" my mom asked, completely ignoring Flash's question.

I avoided her gaze, not knowing what to say.

"You don't know," she said, her face drooping in disappointment. "Is that why you came? To tell me your goodbyes?"

"Of course not, Mom," I said. "It's just that if I go anywhere near Danielle's suspects and someone says I tampered with evidence or claims I was obstructing justice, that will look really bad for you. And it could get me and the kids arrested. Is that what you want?"

My mom's expression drooped a little further. "I suppose not."

Flash set down the paper and pen on the floor, recognizing that he wasn't going to get any names from my mom. "On the bright side, we found Keith's debt collection book." He pulled it from his pocket. "Was he already a loan shark when you knew him?"

My mom's gaze snapped to Flash. And then she laughed.

23

"Keith, a loan shark?" My mom laughed harder. "Where would you get a crazy idea like that?"

My brows knit in confusion. "This book that shows all the people who owe him money. CJ needed me to pick up dad's car, and it was sitting inside on the floor."

"May I?" my mom asked, holding out a hand.

As I slipped it through the bars, Danielle barked, "What are you giving her?"

"Just my dad's old notebook," I said. "I thought she might like to have it."

Danielle made a beeline toward us, but my mom had already snatched the notebook from my fingers.

"If that's evidence, I need to see it," Danielle said.

"I don't know what it is," I said truthfully. "It was in my dad's car when I picked it up from CJ's."

My mom flipped through the pages as fast as she could, knowing Danielle could confiscate it any moment.

"Hand it over," Danielle said, giving my mom her sternest look.

My mom closed the book and handed it to the sheriff. "Fine. But there's nothing useful in there. Abbreviated names next to random dollar amounts." She turned to me. "I don't recognize any of it, but I can tell you that you're wrong about Keith being a loan shark. We were dirt poor, and if he had had any amount of money, trust me, I would have known."

"Well, even if he wasn't a loan shark, it doesn't change the fact that someone wasn't happy with him. The day before he was killed, someone tampered with his car," Flash said. "I think it was so that Grandpa couldn't make a quick getaway."

Both my mom's and the sheriff's gazes snapped to Flash before landing on me.

"Were you going to tell me about this at some point?" the sheriff asked.

I held up my hands. "I just found out myself. CJ asked us to pick up my dad's car this morning. When we did, he said that someone had loosened a couple of bolts and drained the oil. Nothing serious—nothing that would have killed him and Robyn. If the murderer had really wanted them dead, why wouldn't they have cut the brakes or something equally dramatic—something with the chance of doing real harm?"

"I see your point," Danielle said. "It was as if they wanted Keith and Robyn to be stuck here, but only for a little while. It couldn't have taken CJ more than thirty minutes to do what he needed to, an hour if he was being thorough."

An hour. That was long enough to replace the water in Keith's bottle with the acid. But why wouldn't he stop drinking the moment he realized it wasn't H_2O?

"Could the taste of rust remover be at least somewhat hidden by alcohol?" I asked, more to myself than anyone else.

My mom answered. "Would you like me to try it and let you know?"

Sarcasm. She knew how to do it well.

"No, I don't think that will be necessary," I said, my lips twitching up at the edges. "I was just thinking that we've all taken Robyn's word that Keith stopped drinking years ago, but what if he hadn't? Maybe he was just trying to make a good impression while visiting—trying to get back into our good graces—and he hid it by drinking out of that blue water bottle of his."

"It's an idea," Danielle mused. "There are some cheap vodkas that taste a lot like nail polish remover." My mom, Flash, and I all looked at the sheriff in surprise, and her cheeks darkened. "So I've heard," she quickly added. "I haven't received the report on the contents of the bottle from the lab yet, but I'll follow up with them within the hour."

"That still wouldn't prove my innocence," my mom said. "Everyone has been determined to pin Keith's death on me, and now with Robyn's attempted murder..." She trailed off, and her entire body seemed to droop.

I hated seeing my mom like this—dark circles under her eyes, her hair matted from not brushing it. And it had been less than twenty-four hours.

"Mom, why on earth were you at the hotel in the first place? What happened up there?"

Uncertainty flickered across her face. Doubt. A brief moment of hopelessness. And then she slumped onto the cot at the back of the cell.

"She'd called me a few days ago to warn me that she and Keith were coming—said that he had wanted it to be a surprise when they showed up for your wedding. She'd thought it wasn't fair for them to spring something like that on me, so she'd called to give me a heads up."

"And you didn't think to warn me at the same time?" I asked, more annoyed with my mom than I was with Keith and Robyn.

My mom shrugged. "I thought I could convince them not to come—nothing good would come of it. You had made peace with his absence a long time ago. There was no reason to open up old wounds."

"But they came anyway," I said.

She nodded. "Robyn texted me that they'd checked into the hotel, and I decided to try one last time to convince them to leave town before the wedding. I thought

I'd succeeded—Keith said they'd leave, if that was what I wanted. Even made a big show of repacking their bags. Obviously, he lied."

That was why my mom had been so surprised to see them in the reception tent just before the wedding. But it still didn't make sense.

"Cameron has a picture, Mom," I said. "Of you and Robyn laughing together outside the hotel. That doesn't sound like someone who is trying to convince them to leave."

"Excuse me?" Danielle interrupted, placing a hand to her forehead in frustration. "I can't with you two. I just can't. How do you expect me to help if I don't have all the facts?"

I tried to give her my best innocent expression. "I didn't know the picture was important."

"No, you thought it would make your mom look more guilty, so you purposely withheld it from me."

And there was that.

"I was being civil, that's all," my mom insisted. "That was the first time Robyn and I had ever met, and I figured that if I was polite, it would be easier to convince them to go away."

"Didn't exactly work out that way," Danielle said, scribbling something in her notebook.

My mom's gaze dropped to the floor. "No, it didn't. When I went to the hotel to talk to Robyn yesterday, I swear she was alive. She was packing up, saying she'd been receiving ominous phone calls and she needed to leave town. When I tried questioning her further—telling her we could help her—she kicked me out of her room. I was already home when I heard the news that she'd been shot."

When my mom glanced up, there was moisture in her eyes. "I would never have left her if I'd known what was going to happen."

"Why didn't we see you leave the hotel?" Flash asked. "We were waiting for you in the lobby."

My mom's expression opened in surprise. "Why would you do that?"

"Because we saw you go into the hotel."

My mom studied him for a moment, like she didn't think he was telling her everything. "I took the side exit," she finally said. "It took me right out to Las Colinas, where my car was."

"Wouldn't it have been easier to park in front of the hotel? Less walking," Danielle said, looking skeptical. Everyone knew that my mom avoided walking if she could help it. Bad knees.

"Trust me, I tried," my mom said. "Street parking in front of the hotel was full."

This was getting us nowhere.

"There you have it," I told Danielle. "It was a wrong place, wrong time kind of situation. Can you let my mom go now? She's no threat to anyone. I'm assuming your deputy searched my mom's house and didn't find a gun."

My mom exploded onto her feet in a rare burst of energy. "You went through my things? That's an invasion of privacy."

"Murder suspects don't have rights, Laurie." She glanced at me. "And no, we didn't find a gun."

"So, you can't keep her here," I pushed. "Unless you are going to charge her with murder, you have to let her go. You have no witnesses, and no proof."

Danielle looked at me, her gaze sad.

Oh. She might have more than I realized.

"I can keep her up to seventy-two hours before I have to charge her," Danielle said. "And, unfortunately for your mom, I do have physical evidence placing her at the scene of the attempted murder."

My heart dropped, and I didn't dare ask what evidence they had found.

Danielle told me anyway.

"A green chile pepper earring."

I looked at my mom and noticed her bare ears. "Mom?"

My mom's gaze dropped. "I gave the other one to Danielle for analysis, but yes, it was my earring. Everyone in town knows I'm the only one who owns a pair like it."

There had to be a way out of this.

"You can't prove that she lost it yesterday. It could have been before the wedding."

Danielle shook her head, silent.

It was my mom who gave me the bad news.

"Maddie, they found it covered in Robyn's blood."

24

W ell, that wasn't good.

"My earrings don't have backs on them. They're the type with the long hooks, you know," my mom explained further. "I gave Robyn a hug when I first arrived —wanted to comfort her. It must have gotten caught in her hair. She has so much of it."

Maybe, but there was no way to prove that. Not without a statement from Robyn declaring who had actually tried to shoot her.

I turned to Danielle. "You have nothing tying my mom to Keith's death, right? So she's not a murder suspect. Not as long as Robyn is alive."

Danielle hesitated. "I suppose."

My phone rang, and I slipped it from my purse.

Cameron.

I wouldn't normally have answered it, especially at a

time like this, but a nagging feeling told me I should. Just this once.

I stepped away from my mom's cell and turned my back before touching the green phone icon. "Hey, Cam. What's up?" I tried to make it sound as casual as possible, because whatever errands Cameron had suddenly had to do, I was sure they had something to do with the investigation.

"I'm at the hospital," he said, lowering his voice, like someone might overhear. "Robyn is out of surgery and stable, which means she could wake up any minute. I told them I was her brother, and they never questioned it."

"Good thinking," I said. "Do you know where the bullet hit?"

"Just below the collarbone—nothing major was damaged. She'll need some physical therapy, but she'll be fine."

I gave a sigh of relief. "Thank goodness. I'll come to the hospital as soon as I can." A thought occurred to me. "Is Robyn's phone with her at the hospital?"

"No. I asked for any personal effects, and they said she had none, other than the clothes she'd been wearing, and those are long gone. The sheriff took them for analysis. She probably has Robyn's phone as well."

"Or it could still be in the hotel room." Women didn't have the luxury of being able to keep their phone in their pocket. We were lucky if we got pockets at all—at least ones that weren't fake. That meant if I wanted to find

Robyn's phone, I probably needed to be looking for her purse instead.

"It's possible," Cameron said. "You could ask Benji to keep an eye out for it."

"Benji?" I didn't know what he had to do with Robyn's phone.

"Yeah, he stopped by the house when I was dropping Lilly off. He was heading out to a job but left some chocolate chip muffins at the house for you. Sorry, I thought you knew."

"And the job was at the hotel?"

Cameron was quiet for a moment, like he was waiting for someone to pass him in the hall, then said, "Yeah, they called Benji to clean Robyn's room. You guys apparently don't have professional cleaners in this town, which I find a bit concerning. Anyway, he's probably there now."

I frowned, not liking that Cameron knew where Benji was and I didn't. Benji had told me he had jobs lined up for the day, but I hadn't realized they included cleaning up my stepmother's blood.

"Yeah, I did know. I just...forgot. I'll give him a call and see if he's found anything."

Of course, it would be easier to just ask Danielle if she had Robyn's purse. I glanced at her, unsure how I was going to get that information without asking outright. There was no way she would give it to me if she thought it had to do with the investigation.

"Why are you so interested in Robyn's phone?" Cameron asked.

I took a step towards Danielle's desk and lowered my voice further. "My mom mentioned that Robyn received threatening phone calls yesterday and that she'd been packing up, ready to bolt out of town. If we can get access to her phone, Flash can find where those calls came from. That boy is so good at what he does, we could have my mom home for dinner."

"Okay. I'll stay here with Robyn so I can be here when she wakes up. If you don't find her phone, Robyn's memory might be the only chance we have at finding who did this."

No pressure or anything.

I hung up and turned back to the expectant gazes of the sheriff, my mom, and Flash.

"Well?" Danielle asked when I didn't immediately offer the details of my conversation with Cameron. "I heard you mention Robyn's hotel room. Is Cameron there right now?"

I shook my head. "No, he's not. I guess they've called Benji in to deep clean the room because he has tools the hotel doesn't. Benji usually silences his phone when on a job, and Cameron didn't want me to worry."

"That's very considerate, considering the relationship you have with your ex-husband," Danielle said, her words slow. She wasn't buying it, but she didn't have proof to the contrary.

"It was," I said, then turned to my mom. "I'm going to head out and see if Benji needs food. He never takes enough breaks and ends up forgetting to eat. Do you need anything before I go?"

Danielle was eyeing me with suspicion, and it didn't diminish when my mom smiled and said, "No, I think I'm all right for now. Knowing you didn't abandon me is enough to keep me going. If you happen to see a large key ring with the words 'jail cell' on your way out, though, feel free to toss it my way."

I laughed, hoping it didn't appear too forced. "Of course."

As I approached the sheriff's desk, my steps slowed, my gaze scanning the area around it. I doubted I'd get lucky enough to find Robyn's purse out in the open and within snatching distance, but a woman could try. Imagine my excitement when that was exactly what I found. There, on the floor, was a purse. It was dark green with gold embroidered flowers across the front.

I glanced back and saw that Flash was taking his sweet time, though whether it was on purpose or not, I wasn't sure. I loved Flash, but he was the most easily distractible person I knew.

In this case, it was exactly what I needed.

I bent down next to the desk, untying my shoelace as I did so. I reached for the purse, but before I could grab it, Danielle walked up next to me, her hands on her hips and a look of strong disapproval on her face.

"Something you need, Maddie?"

Flash joined her, his gaze curious.

"Just tying my shoe," I said, pointing to the untied lace. "My mom always tells me I should use a double knot, but they're so annoying to undo." I quickly tied the shoe and straightened. "We'll be back later, Mom," I called across the room. "Don't give Danielle too much trouble. She's just doing her job."

"If she were doing her job, she'd have never arrested me in the first place," my mom called back.

I gave Danielle a smile and a look that said, *What can you do?*

"I'm serious when I say that you need to tell me if you know anything that can help me with this case," Danielle said as she walked us to the door. "I'm very good at my job, and everything points to your mom doing it. She has strong motive in the murder of your dad, and she can be placed at the scene of the attempted murder of your step-mom. Everyone else has an alibi. It's not looking good."

"Victor Bailey had a doctor's appointment near the church a couple hours before the wedding," I pointed out.

Danielle's lips parted in surprise. "How did you—" She shook her head. "Never mind. I don't want to know." She glanced toward the cell at the other side of the room. "I talked with Victor and his doctor. Their stories match up. We also have video footage of Victor driving past the church towards home, after his appointment. He never returns. Video footage from a neighbor's doorbell camera shows a woman from a meal service delivering food to him about twenty minutes after he arrived home.

She handed it to him personally. There was no way he did it."

Darn.

I liked the guy, and I felt sorry for him, but if I had a choice between my mom and him being the murderer, I knew what I would decide. Every time.

"Okay," I said, feeling dejected. That was another suspect down. We were running out of them.

Danielle touched my arm. "I'm really trying my best here, Maddie. Believe it or not, I like your mom."

I nodded, avoiding her gaze. The one that held pity and made me feel worse than I already did.

"I know." I glanced at her. "Have you looked into Karla, over at the hotel?"

Danielle tilted her head, like she was wondering why I was asking. "I've talked to her a couple of times to gain access to the hotel's video footage."

"And?"

Danielle lifted a shoulder. "And the security cameras were down. They didn't capture anything."

"You don't find that suspicious?"

"Of course I do," Danielle said. "And I've interviewed every employee and security guard at the hotel. Before you ask, Karla has an alibi—she was helping out at the front desk of the hotel when Robyn was shot. Everyone backs up her story."

"But she was literally in the same location that—"

Danielle held up a hand, her brows furrowing in frustration. "Stop, Maddie. Just stop. This is my job, so please, for once, let me do it."

I held her gaze for a moment before spinning away. "Fine."

And then I left with Flash, wondering how we were ever going to get my mom out of this.

WHEN WE ARRIVED at the hotel to check in with Benji, no one stopped us from entering, as I had expected they would, considering our last run-in with Karla. I didn't know where these security guards were that Danielle had claimed worked there, but I was grateful they weren't interested in me. Flash and I took the elevator straight up to the fourth floor and followed the sound of the shop vac. When I peeked in, Benji was running the nozzle over a small patch of blood. It had been soaked with cleaning solution, and the liquid he was pulling out was bright red.

My stomach lurched, and I had to force myself to stay.

Benji used one hand to wipe sweat from his forehead, his white T-shirt already soaked through. I had never understood why he didn't wear darker colors when he worked. Sure, the white was cooler for outside, but it got dirty so fast. The view wasn't bad, though. I always forgot how strong he was, his abs showing through the wet fabric.

And I was the lucky woman who got to have those abs all to herself.

"Mom, stop looking at him like that," Flash half-shouted so he could be heard above the noise of the shop vac. "It's gross."

Benji heard and glanced in our direction, grinning. He turned the vacuum off. "This is a nice surprise. How did you know I would be here?"

"Cameron, of all people," I said. "Why didn't you call me to let me know you would be here?"

Benji raised a shoulder, looking embarrassed at the oversight. "I figured you were busy. Lilly told me you'd gone to the sheriff's office to visit your mom, and I didn't want to interrupt."

Always the gentleman, even when he shouldn't be. "Well, you still should have called," I said. "You get something to eat before you came over?"

Benji nodded. "Stopped by the diner. I left some muffins at the house for you." He paused. "How's your mom doing?"

"About as well as can be expected, but I hate seeing her like this. I wish there was more I could do."

Benji stepped around the bloodstain and pulled me into a hug, his sweat making my own shirt damp. "There are still other suspects—"

"No, there aren't," I interrupted. "The only one left is Karla, and the sheriff doesn't seem interested in looking at her at all. Said that Karla has an ironclad alibi."

Benji stepped back. "I'm sorry. I know how frustrating that must be for you."

I wiped at a stray tear on my cheek. I hadn't even realized I'd been crying.

Benji kissed me on the forehead, then turned his attention to Flash. "Mind helping me lift the bed? I'm going to need to clean under there, just in case...you know..."

"The blood splattered," Flash finished for him. "Yeah, no problem."

I hated how comfortable Flash was with this kind of stuff—I still wasn't used to it, despite all the predicaments my family had gotten into over the years. I forced my gaze away from the blood-soaked carpet and onto Benji. "Want to go out for lunch when you're done here?"

Benji threw me a smile. "Of course."

Flash took the side of the bed that was closest to the wall, and Benji took the opposite.

"Count of three," Benji said, "One...two...three..."

They lifted together, grunting under the weight of what appeared to be a solid wood bedframe.

"Why didn't we take the mattress off first?" Flash asked, sweat beading his forehead.

They both gave a final heave, and the bed frame turned onto its side.

"Forgot," Benji said, wiping his face.

And that was when I saw it.

A phone, sitting in the middle of the floor where the bed had sat.

25

I leaped toward the phone. My foot hit the edge of the bed frame, and it swayed. I threw my arms over my head, anticipating impact, but Flash and Benji grabbed the edges before it could crash down on top of me.

"Maddie, what in the world are you doing?" Benji asked, his voice laced with panic. "You could have been seriously injured."

I grabbed the phone. "I don't know if this was Keith's or Robyn's, but I don't even care. Whether it helps us find who was threatening Robyn or gives us more information on what was going on with this loan shark business, it could lead us to my dad's real killer."

"Everyone says there's no way Keith could have been a loan shark," Flash said. "He didn't have the resources to lend people money—he was the one who owed everyone else money."

I crawled backwards, out of range of another near-accident, and pressed the button on the side of the phone, waking it up. I was stopped from going any further when it asked for a passcode.

Why had I thought I knew what to do with this? I held it out to Flash.

"If my dad wasn't involved in shady business, then why does he have a burner phone?" I asked.

Flash stared. "Seriously?"

I waved it in the air, waiting for him to take it from me. "Here, break into it."

"It isn't that easy, Mom. If he was here using the phone, I could easily hack in using the free Wi-Fi, then I'd plant something and use that to pull information off of it. But without someone already having access to it, the only ways I know to bypass his passcode would erase all his data."

"Which would defeat the point of all of this," I finished. "So, you need to find another way. Your grandma's freedom is at stake here, and the only thing stopping us is a six-digit number."

Flash took the phone from my hands. "I doubt Grandpa would be this dumb, but maybe he used his or Robyn's birthdate. What is Grandpa's birthday?"

"I have no idea."

Benji glanced over at me as he sprayed carpet cleaner where the bed had been, using his back to prop the frame upright. "If it's Keith's phone, it could be your birthday. Who knows, maybe he was sentimental."

I highly doubted it and wasn't surprised when Flash quickly typed in the numbers, then shook his head. "Nope." He typed again. "It's not Grandma's birthday either."

"I don't know anything about either of these people," I said, burying my face in my hands. "So close and yet—"

Flash released a celebratory yell and punched a fist in the air, making me jump.

"You got in?" I asked. "How?"

Flash shook his head. "Nope. But you know how you can see a preview of missed calls, texts, emails, and all that on your lock screen?"

I nodded, embarrassed. I hadn't even thought to look at those when I'd tried getting into the phone—just ignored them while jumping ahead to the impossible six-digit code.

"Grandpa has received twenty-four missed calls since someone last accessed this phone."

"Who are they from?" I asked. Twenty-four calls meant that someone was desperate to talk to my dad.

Flash looked at me like I was crazy. "The point of a burner phone is to not be connected to anyone—you don't want other people knowing what you're doing and who you're talking to. Grandpa wouldn't have saved anyone in his address book."

I took the phone from Flash and scrolled through the lock screen. "Half of these missed calls are from the same person."

"Think that's our murderer?" Benji asked, leaning on the bed frame.

"Maybe..." But even as I said it, I didn't think so. Something wasn't adding up here.

I sprang to my feet. "Flash, you're staying here and helping Benji. I need to go meet Cameron at the hospital. Robyn will be waking up any minute now, and I have some questions that need answering."

"But—" Flash began to protest.

I held up a finger and used my best mom voice. "I'm serious, Flash. Stay here. I'll call your sister and let her know where everyone is."

And then I threw the burner phone into my purse and ran out the door before anyone could stop me.

I TRIED CALLING Lilly as I drove the three miles to the hospital located at the outskirts of town.

No answer.

I then tried Cameron to ask if Robyn had woken yet.

Nothing.

My mind raced as I drove, trying to piece together everything that had happened in the past couple of days, but it was like trying to put together a two-sided jigsaw puzzle—you weren't sure which shapes and colors belonged with which picture, and even as you put it together, you wondered if it was all wrong.

I rolled up to a stoplight—the only one in Amor. While

I waited for the light to turn green, I slipped the burner phone out of my purse and pulled up the lock screen. I scrolled through the entire list of missed calls, hoping I'd catch a lucky break. Both Flash and I had done a quick scan of the numbers, but we could have missed something.

It turned out we had.

When I reached the end of all twenty-four missed calls, at the bottom was a single text message.

My heart fell.

And then I called the sheriff. She was the third person in the past five minutes to not answer their phone. It seemed everyone was avoiding me today, so I left a message.

I really needed her to be at the hospital when Robyn woke up.

WHEN I WALKED into Robyn's room, my chest constricted. Robyn was awake, smiling and joking with Cameron as he held her hand. And Lilly was there, pouring Robyn a cup of water.

"I tried calling you," I told Lilly. "You didn't answer."

She smiled as she handed Robyn the cup. "Sorry. Dad called me and said he was going stir-crazy—wanted to know if I wanted to wait with him at the hospital." She nodded to a small table where a deck of cards sat. "An hour after I arrived, Robyn woke. She's doing amazing, all things considered."

Robyn gave her a weak smile. "I had nothing to do with that." She looked at me. "I hear that you called 911. I owe you my life."

"Anyone would have done it," I said, approaching the bed. I tried to smile, but it wasn't convincing anyone.

Robyn mistook my dread for sadness. "It's been a traumatic couple of days for you, hasn't it," she said kindly, patting my hand.

I nodded. "Terrible. It almost feels like the universe is conspiring against me, determined to not give me my happily-ever-after." I glanced at Cameron. "No offense."

"Some taken," he said. "But what matters is that Robyn is awake and is expected to make a full recovery."

"Absolutely." I turned back to Robyn. "I hate to bring this up at a time like this, but did you see who shot you? The sooner the sheriff arrests who did it, the sooner we can all rest easy knowing they can't hurt anyone else."

Because even though I felt like the pieces were starting to click together and I was finally able to tell which side of the puzzle which pieces belonged to, this was still one piece that was missing—one piece that didn't make sense.

"Karla shot Robyn," Danielle said, walking into the room. "When you mentioned the hotel manager and I told you that her story checked out, I realized that even though everyone swears they saw her at the time of the murder, she was constantly on the move as she helped their guests, and no one was really sure of the precise moment they saw her. I had my deputy do a more thorough search of the hotel."

"And he found something," I said.

Danielle nodded. "He recovered a gun from a dumpster behind the hotel. It was wrapped in Karla's cardigan." She glanced at me. "You'll be happy to know that we've released your mom, and Karla is now the occupant of her jail cell. We're running fingerprints on the gun now."

I knew I had said that it had to be Karla—she certainly had motive—but this felt too easy. A gun wrapped in her cardigan and sitting in the hotel's dumpster? Why hadn't she just walked down to the sheriff's station and turned herself in? It would have been easier and produced the same result.

"Oh, thank goodness you caught her before she escaped town," Robyn said, releasing a relieved sigh. "Keith told me about her before we came out here—wanted to warn me. 'Unhinged' is what he said. I thought he was exaggerating, but to attack us both like that? Well, I owe my life to Maddie and her family."

Danielle's gaze lingered on me as Robyn spoke. "You don't look happy that we caught your dad's murderer. Why?"

My mind began clicking through everything we knew, everything that wasn't settling right. Robyn couldn't have shot herself. It was impossible. Someone had to have done it. Why not Karla?

"Your car was tampered with after you arrived in Amor," I told Robyn. "After you checked into the hotel."

Robyn nodded. "That's right. CJ was kind enough to look at it and said he was a bit backed up, but that he'd get that oil changed and the bolts tightened as soon as he could. A real sweetheart."

"Karla would have had access to their car at the hotel," Lilly pointed out.

"True," I said. "But how would she have access to oxalic acid?"

Robyn raised a finger. "It's in a lot of bleaches, and there's plenty of that at the hotel."

I glanced at Danielle. "Did you ever get the report back on what was actually in the water bottle?"

She shifted uncomfortably, as though realizing things weren't as cut and dried as they'd first appeared. "A combination of alcohol and rust cleaner."

"Not bleach," I said. "And certainly not water." I glanced at Robyn. "My dad hadn't stopped drinking, had he?"

She hesitated, her gaze finally dropping. "He tried—he really did. But he just couldn't do it."

"So, for appearance's sake, he carried that water bottle wherever he went," I said. "If Karla had thought his bottle contained water, wouldn't she realize that as soon as my dad opened it, he'd smell the cleaner?"

Robyn gave a slow nod. "I guess."

"But cheap vodka—that can cover up a bit more, can't

it? And there was only one person who knew what was actually in that bottle—one person who had access to rust remover when she and her husband dropped their car off at CJ's." I glanced at Robyn. "It was convenient that your car had been tampered with. Nothing life threatening, mind you, but enough that it would need to spend at least a couple of hours in the shop."

Cameron's lips parted in surprise. "You're not seriously suggesting that Robyn killed your dad."

Robyn tried to look equally surprised, but it was her eyes that I was watching. When they hardened, I knew I was on the right track.

"Maddie," Danielle said, touching my sleeve. Her voice was soft, but it held warning. "I think you need to leave now—you're too emotionally invested."

"I'm not—"

Danielle cut me off, her tone firm. "Robyn is a victim." She paused. "I understand how frustrating it is that you can no longer have the closure you needed with your father. But now you're projecting all that hurt and anger from your childhood trauma onto his new wife. It's under-standable, but it's not okay. Especially not in these circumstances. Robyn didn't kill Keith, and it was impos-sible for her to shoot herself at the angle the bullet entered."

What did the sheriff know about childhood trauma and projecting? I'd always said she'd make a great psychol-ogist, but she'd just crossed the line.

I pulled in three long breaths as I tried to calm myself enough to respond.

"Oh, I know Robyn didn't shoot herself," I said. "But being a loan shark, that's a dangerous business, isn't it? My dad, he never had the money to do something like that, as I've been told countless times." I met Robyn's gaze. "But then you came along and were the answer to all his problems. All his debts. His inability to keep a job. Maybe he didn't care how you made your money at first. Heck, you probably even kept it secret from him."

Robyn's eyes narrowed, but she didn't say anything.

"Maddie," Danielle said again, the warning in her tone not so subtle this time.

"Hear her out," Lilly said. "It makes sense. The notebook we found in the car with all the names and dollar amounts—we assumed it belonged to Grandpa because it was his car. But we found it on the floor on the passenger side."

"And then there's this," I said, pulling the burner phone from my pocket.

Robyn's expression transformed from anger to shock. And then fear. "Where did you get that?" she whispered.

"My fiancé is currently cleaning blood out of your hotel room's carpet," I said, tossing the phone into the air and catching it. "Found this under the bed. You've missed a lot of calls."

"Let me see that," Danielle said, and I handed it to her.

"You'll be particularly interested in the last text message."

Robyn tried pushing herself up into a sitting position, but she collapsed back onto the bed, her face contorted in pain. "You're lying. No one texts me on that phone."

"Looks like someone broke the rules," I said. "Apparently, you've threatened a man's wife if you don't receive payment. He doesn't sound very happy about that. Looks like he has a lot of threats of his own."

26

I handed Danielle the burner phone. She glanced at it, then turned to Robyn. "What's the passcode?"

Robyn remained silent, and she was suddenly far too interested in her fingernails.

"Things will go much better for you if you cooperate," Danielle said. "I can only help you if you help me."

More silence.

Danielle shrugged. "Suit yourself." She called out to her deputy, who was waiting in the hallway. When Danielle handed the phone to him, Robyn's eyes grew wide with panic, and her heart was beating so hard and fast, the machine she was hooked up to went crazy and two nurses ran into the room.

"She just got out of surgery, and she needs rest," one of them said, scolding us, while the other silenced the machine and then placed an oxygen mask on Robyn's face, instructing her to take deep breaths. "Your questions are upsetting her. They will need to wait."

This couldn't wait. Not when we were so close to a confession.

Danielle was on the same wavelength and shook her head. "It's Robyn who's making this hard on herself, not me. I'll leave as soon as we either get the information we need off her phone or she cooperates. It's her choice."

Robyn's heartrate had steadied, and she weakly took the oxygen mask off.

"Fine. It doesn't matter now. What do you want to know?"

I SAT on the cold floor in the hospital hallway, my back against the wall. Robyn's confession played on repeat in my mind.

Yes, Keith had still had a drinking problem, but yes, he really had wanted to come to my wedding to make amends.

No, my father hadn't wanted Robyn there. What he'd wanted was a divorce. He'd enjoyed the benefits of her life-style, but that hadn't been enough anymore. He'd still believed in a silly thing called love, and it had been missing from their marriage for some time now.

And Robyn couldn't have that—not with everything he knew about her business dealings. Divorce wasn't an option. Not when he was married to a loan shark.

Yes, she had drained the oil from the car and loosened the bolts. Yes, she had stolen rust cleaner and added just enough to my dad's water bottle that he shouldn't notice.

And finally, no, she didn't regret it.

Robyn's hospital door opened, interrupting my thoughts, and I glanced up to see Danielle looking down at me.

She walked over and slid onto the floor next to me.

"You okay?"

I released a humorless laugh. "No. Not at all."

Danielle nodded, then pulled her knees to her chest. Her gaze remained fixed on the floor.

"Are Cameron and Lilly still here?" she asked.

"No. I sent them home. Everyone's meeting up at the house later today for a party to celebrate my mom's release, but I need a little more time before I join them."

Danielle shifted, trying to get comfortable on the hard floor. "Understandable."

I glanced at her. "Did Karla actually shoot Robyn? Just from the limited amount I know about her, I can't imagine it."

Danielle's lips lifted at the corners. "No, and she was never under serious suspicion, even though I have to admit that the time and place everything happened was terrible luck on her part."

I stared at Danielle. Just when I thought I knew her, she did something to surprise me. "But you found the gun with Karla's..." My words trailed off because

Danielle wore a guilty expression. "That never happened, did it."

Danielle shook her head. "No. The thing was, even though I didn't have reason to suspect Robyn of killing Keith, not with her being shot like that, something felt off. I heard there had been an awkward encounter when Robyn and Keith had checked into the hotel—Karla had been the one to help them. Because I knew that Robyn knew who Karla was, I decided to see if she would correct me when I said that it had been Karla who had shot her."

"And she didn't," I said. "She was more than happy for Karla to take the fall. Was that to protect herself?"

"Probably. She didn't know the woman who shot her—never seen her before. For all she knew, the woman was the wife she'd been threatening if the husband didn't pay what he owed. Couldn't have me digging into all that, could she."

I cocked my head to the side, studying Danielle. "You know who shot Robyn, don't you."

Danielle nodded, but her gaze dropped.

It was someone I knew.

My pulse quickened, and I struggled to breathe. "If you lied about arresting Karla, that means my mom is still locked up."

Danielle looked at me with a horrified expression. "Oh my gosh, no. I'm sorry, I should have made that clearer. Your mother did not shoot Robyn, and she really has been released."

If I thought I could have gotten away with hitting Danielle in the arm right then, I would have. But I hadn't forgotten that she was still the sheriff, and she could still arrest me, even if she was my friend. Most of the time.

"That was evil," I said.

She shook her head. "I know. I'm sorry."

When Danielle still didn't reveal who the shooter had been, I raised an eyebrow. "Well?" She hesitated, as if she wasn't certain she was allowed to tell me. I held up a threatening finger. "After what you just did, you owe me."

"I suppose I do." Her gaze slid along the hallway, making sure no one else was listening in. "It was the woman who delivers Victor Bailey's meals. Cindy."

I stared. "What?"

Danielle raised a shoulder. "I know. That was my reaction too. But apparently, after four years of her visiting his home twice a day, she and Victor became good friends. Victor saw your dad standing outside the church as he drove home from his doctor's appointment, and when Cindy brought him his lunch, he was fuming about Keith having the guts to return to their town after what he'd done. She knew what had happened to his son, and she made an off-the-cuff comment about Victor needing to hire someone to send Keith to hell, because that was the only place he would get what he deserved."

"Victor's lunch lady offered to kill someone for him? Who does that?" I asked, incredulous.

"I don't think Cindy meant for Victor to hire her,"

Danielle said. "I don't know if she was even serious. But Victor took her suggestion seriously, and he knew this would be the only chance he'd ever have. He offered her ten thousand dollars on the spot to take care of it that afternoon."

I blinked. "And she did it, just like that."

"Cindy was having her own money problems, and ten thousand dollars would take care of all of them. She told me that she felt bad about taking Victor's money—it was his life savings—but he convinced her that she needed it more than he did, and if it meant there was one less monster in the world, why not?"

I shook my head, still not believing what I was hearing. "This is unreal." My gaze snapped to Danielle. "But she didn't kill my dad. When she shot Robyn, my dad had already been dead for several hours. Why did she do it?"

Danielle gave me a sad smile. "Neither Cindy nor Victor was at the wedding, remember? She was doing deliveries, and Victor was home plotting his revenge. Victor didn't know that Keith had remarried, so when the hotel door opened..."

"Cindy shot Robyn by accident," I finished for her, and then I buried my head in my hands. "This isn't normal. These types of things don't happen to other people. I'm cursed, and so is everyone around me. It's my fault that my dad is dead and Robyn was shot—because that's just what happens when you've been exposed to Maddie Swallows."

Danielle snorted. "Please, you don't get to take credit

for everything that happens in your life. Maybe these things occur when you're around because the universe knows you have the mind and heart to help bring justice to those who need it. Maybe you're exactly where you're supposed to be, at exactly the right time. You ever think of that?"

I hadn't, and I wasn't sure I believed it.

I pushed myself off the floor and then held out a hand to Danielle to help her up. "I suppose I should be getting home so I can clean myself up before the party. You want to come? After the past two days, you deserve it."

Danielle used my hand to pull herself to her feet, then brushed off her pants. "Thanks, but you wouldn't believe the amount of paperwork that one murder and one attempted murder create. It will take me twice as long as it did to solve the case."

"I guess I'll see you after my honeymoon, then," I said. "Assuming Benji hasn't gotten cold feet. This hasn't been the best start to our nearly married life."

"That man is so madly in love, you could be the one convicted of murder and he'd still marry you."

This time I did hit Danielle in the arm. "You can't say stuff like that," I whispered. "That universe you were talking about that puts me in just the right place and time —it heard you, and now you've jinxed me."

Danielle laughed. "I'm sure you'll be fine. Those types of things only sometimes come true."

I wasn't sure I liked those odds.

EPILOGUE

I knew that throwing my mom a Welcome Home From Jail party was what she needed, but as soon as people started showing up, I wondered if it had been a mistake. Maybe we should have waited another day to let things settle.

By the time I felt emotionally ready to descend the stairs and join everyone, the party was already in full swing. Well, as much as the Swallows family knew how to party. Flash was telling everyone that removing blood from carpet wasn't as exciting as he'd thought it would be, and Lilly kept interrupting, wanting to make sure everyone knew she'd actually been there for Robyn's confession. Flash wouldn't let her talk, though, probably jealous he hadn't been at the hospital.

The living room and kitchen were full of friends and

neighbors, and I could see that the back door was open, with even more people mingling in the backyard.

Cameron walked up to me, a drink in hand. "How are you feeling? All's well that ends well, right?"

"I guess," I said. "Robyn will be going to prison, where she belongs, but I hope the jury goes easy on Victor." When Cameron raised an eyebrow, I recognized the irony of it. "I'm aware that he intended to kill my father, but can you blame the guy?"

Cameron laughed and shook his head. "That's why I fell in love with you—your good heart. I can't say I was blessed with the same quality."

"I agree with everything you just said," Benji said, walking up behind me and wrapping his arms around my waist. "Both that her good heart and honest nature are two of her most beautiful attributes, and that you, Cameron, do not possess them." He said it with a grin, like he was teasing Cameron.

Was it possible those two were getting along?

That was a little too weird for me.

Cameron laughed, not taking offense, and merely shrugged in resignation. "It's true." He glanced between us. "So, what are your plans? You still getting married or what?"

Benji stepped out from behind me and took my hand. His gaze met mine. "I hope you don't mind me taking the lead on this, but the resort in Colorado said they could shift our reservation by three days, and they have a chapel on-site if we wanted to be married there. I know it won't be the same without Flash and Lilly, but—"

"No way. I'm not allowing that to happen," Cameron said. "The kids need to be at your wedding, especially after everything they've been through."

I was about to chastise him for interfering—this was absolutely none of his business—but he disappeared into the crowd before I had the chance.

"I know they'd prefer to be there, but they'll understand," I told Benji. "We can't put this wedding off any longer."

Trish appeared at my side, my wedding dress draped over her arms. "I couldn't agree more. You cannot put off this wedding, even if you have been avoiding my calls for the past two days and no one answered the door when I stopped by the house. I thought you'd died."

"Trish," I said, dropping Benji's hand and wrapping her in a hug. "I'm so sorry. I should have called you back but—"

Trish held up a hand. "I'm going to stop you there. You do not need to apologize to me, but you do need to put on this dress. Your ex-husband is gathering everyone in the backyard, and Pastor Franks said he is prepared to marry you two, if you are ready."

Just seeing the dress made my chest constrict. Panic flooded over me, and I took a step back. "I'm sorry, I just don't think I can get married in that dress. Not again."

Rather than looking disappointed, Trish grinned. "I

thought you might say that." She unceremoniously tossed the wedding dress aside, and it landed on the couch, one of the sleeves falling into someone's red punch. Underneath the dress, still draped on Trish's arms, were my flannel pajamas.

"I washed and ironed them so they'd be ready for your big day, whenever that happened to be," she said. "But I totally understand if that isn't today. If you're not ready, don't do it."

I looked at Benji. "All of our friends and family are here today. We have food, music. What do you think?"

Benji grinned and took my hands in his. "I think you better change clothes. Because we're getting married today."

THIS WASN'T how I had envisioned getting married. There were no chairs in my backyard, no flowers, and Benji had to remove a rattlesnake before we could begin.

As soon as I walked outside and my mom saw what I was wearing, she said, "Honestly, Maddie. You're really going to get married wearing flannel, aren't you."

Yes, I was.

And I'd never felt more beautiful.

Flash and Lilly waited for me at the end of the rock path, where Benji stood, and I immediately started crying. I didn't even try to stop it this time, because there was no makeup to smudge.

Today was about the important things—what was real.

And my family and friends gathered here, crammed in my backyard drinking soda and eating all the leftover chicken salad sandwiches from Benji and my failed wedding reception, was real.

At my request, Pastor Franks skipped to the vows. The quicker we could get through this ceremony, the more likely nothing terrible would happen to interrupt it.

Benji took my hands in his. "Maddie, we've been partners in crime since the second grade when we discovered Ms. Markus's secret stash of snacks. There have been ups and downs since then, but I don't regret a moment of it. When I'm with you, I sing louder, cook better, love more, and I can't imagine spending another second of my life without you, Flash, or Lilly." He paused. "Of course, I've also become far more acquainted with the inner workings of law enforcement than I ever thought I would—or wanted to be."

Everyone laughed at that, including me, though the tears were coming so hard now, I couldn't see.

"I love you, Maddie," he finished, his voice soft.

It was my turn.

And there were so many things I wanted to say. I wanted to tell Benji that he was the one who kept me grounded when I was feeling crazy. How he made me laugh when all I wanted to do was cry. How I had given up on love before he'd come back into my life. How I was so grateful for the father he'd been to Flash and Lilly through their teenage years, even when he hadn't needed to be.

But I couldn't say any of it.

Instead, I wrapped him in a hug and whispered in his ear, "Thank you for being you. I don't need or want anything more than that. You're perfect."

And then my words became so incomprehensible, I stopped trying.

Pastor Franks rushed through the rest where we both said "I do," probably because of all the crying. All I really needed was for him to say, "I now pronounce you man and wife." It was the only part I cared about. That, and the kissing.

And I got both.

Benji pulled me into his arms as everyone cheered. "We leave first thing in the morning for Colorado. Think you can handle being alone with me for an entire week? I know it will be the longest you've gone without Flash and Lilly since...ever."

I leaned back and smiled, the tears finally slowing. "I think I can probably manage spending a week with the love of my life, relaxing in hot tubs and taking in the mountain air while people bring us our drinks on pretty trays."

Benji returned my smile, but he also looked a bit guilty.

"Why does your face look like that?" I asked, straightening.

"We are going to a resort in Colorado," he said, his words slow, "but it's not that kind of resort."

"What other kind is there?" I asked, dread settling in my stomach.

"I got a great discount," he started, no longer meeting my gaze. "I know a guy who knows a guy sort of thing. There will definitely be beautiful mountains, and I'm pretty sure there's a hot tub—"

"What kind of resort is it?" I asked again, getting more nervous by the minute.

Benji hesitated. "The Old Western kind."

I didn't even know what that meant.

My expression must have shown it, so Benji continued. "It's an immersive experience where you feel like you're living in an old Western movie. There will be gunfights, bank robberies, and a tour of a ghost town. The works. Our room is in one of the most coveted buildings—it sits above the saloon and has an amazing view of the entire town. You're going to love it."

He looked like he was trying to convince himself more than me.

I didn't want him to feel bad about what he'd chosen for our honeymoon—even if I did feel misled. I knew he'd tried. So I kissed him.

"Sounds awesome, as long as the cowboys are firing blanks. I need a break from real murder for a week."

Relief washed across Benji's face, and it made me

smile. He was so dang cute, I would follow him anywhere if it meant I got a week alone with him.

"I promise, only fake murders allowed."

That was a promise I was going to hold him to.

The End

CHOOSE YOUR OWN ADVENTURE: MYSTERY OR ROMANCE

MADDIE SWALLOWS MYSTERIES

Dead Before Dinner

Dead Upon Arrival

Dead Before I Do

Dead Among Stars

Dead by Design

Dead in the Dark

Dead Without a Hitch

Dead by the Outlaw's Noose

BORROWING AMOR: New Mexican Romance

Borrowing Amor

Borrowing Love

Borrowing a Fiancé

Borrowing a Billionaire

Borrowing Kisses

Borrowing Second Chances

STARLIGHT RIDGE: Beach Romance

Diving into Love

ABOUT THE AUTHOR

Kat Bellemore is the author of both the Borrowing Amor small town romance series and the Maddie Swallows cozy mystery series. Deciding to have New Mexico as the setting for these series was an easy choice, considering its amazing sunsets, blue skies and tasty green chile. That, and she currently lives there with her husband and two cute kids. They hope to one day add a dog to the family, but for now, the native animals of the desert will have to do. Though, Kat wouldn't mind ridding the world of scorpions and centipedes. They're just mean.

You can visit Kat at www.kat-bellemore.com.